FELL BACK

BOOKS BY M. E. KERR

Dinky Hocker Shoots Smack!
Best of the Best Books (YA) 1970–83 (ALA)
Best Children's Books of 1972, *School Library Journal*
ALA Notable Children's Books of 1972

If I Love You, Am I Trapped Forever?
Honor Book, *Book World* Children's Spring Book Festival, 1973
Outstanding Children's Books of 1973, *The New York Times*

The Son of Someone Famous
(An Ursula Nordstrom Book)
Best Children's Books of 1974, *School Library Journal*
"Best of the Best" Children's Books, 1966–1978, *School Library Journal*

Is That You, Miss Blue?
(An Ursula Nordstrom Book)
Outstanding Children's Books of 1975, *The New York Times*
ALA Notable Children's Books of 1975
Best Books for Young Adults, 1975 (ALA)

Love Is a Missing Person
(An Ursula Nordstrom Book)

I'll Love You When You're More Like Me
(An Ursula Nordstrom Book)
Best Children's Books of 1977, *School Library Journal*

Gentlehands
(An Ursula Nordstrom Book)
Best Books for Young Adults, 1978 (ALA)
ALA Notable Children's Books of 1978
Best Children's Books of 1978, *School Library Journal*

M.E. KERR

FELL BACK

HARPER & ROW, PUBLISHERS NEW YORK
Grand Rapids, Philadelphia, St. Louis, San Francisco, London
Singapore, Sydney, Tokyo, Toronto

Fell Back

 Printed in the United States of America. For information address Harper & Row Junior Books, 10 East 53rd Street, New York, N.Y. 10022.
Typography by Joyce Hopkins
1 2 3 4 5 6 7 8 9 10
First Edition

Library of Congress Cataloging-in-Publication Data
Kerr, M. E.
Fell back.

"A Charlotte Zolotow book."
Summary: When a classmate at his exclusive private school falls to his death from a tower, seventeen-year-old John Fell is determined to find out whether the incident was suicide, accident, or murder.
[1. Schools—Fiction. 2. Mystery and detective stories] I. Title.
PZ7.K46825Fg 1989 [Fic] 88-35762
ISBN 0-06-023292-7
ISBN 0-06-023293-5

TO ALEX AND CALI COLE:

"A TOUCH OF LOVE."

1

ABOUT TWO WEEKS AFTER I returned to Gardner, one cold Wednesday afternoon, there was a crowd gathered down by The Tower. I jogged that way to see what all the excitement was about. There were snowdrifts all around. We'd hit a record for bad weather in January.

"Fell. Hurry, Fell!" Dib shouted at me.

I pushed my way toward him, and before I got to the front of the crowd, Dib said, "It's Lasher! He jumped from the top!"

Someone else said, "He finally did it!"

Dib turned and told me, "He's committed suicide, Fell!"

I stood there beside Dib, looking down at the cold pavement.

Beside Lasher's body, I saw his thick glasses with the panes smashed.

Then in less time than it takes a paper clip to inch over to a magnet, I said, "No. He didn't kill himself."

Those five words were going to get me into a lot of trouble.

◻

"No one who knows he is about to get a new Porsche for his birthday kills himself," said Lasher's father.

His sister said, "Oh, come *on*, Daddy! He *gave* his VCR away, his watch, the Mont Blanc pen you bought him for Christmas. He was planning it!"

I watched the snow fall outside my window in Sevens House.

"Why didn't he even leave a note?" Dr. Lasher shook his bald head sadly.

"Because he wasn't in control of himself, Daddy. You saw how he was at Christmas—never smiling, always sleeping."

"He said nothing about suicide, however."

"He said nothing. Period. He wouldn't talk to anyone."

"Paul was often moody and melancholy."

"Not like that, no, never."

"Are you listening, Fell?" Dr. Lasher asked.

I glanced across at him. He bore a faint resemblance to his late son. He had the same bad eyesight, too.

"Yes, sir," I said. "You don't think it was suicide. I heard you."

"I know it was," his daughter said. "I knew him better than anyone."

No one would argue with that. Lauren was Lasher's twin. "Poised" would not describe her adequately. "Conceited" would be going too far. She was somewhere in between. Miss Tyler's School, over in Princeton, New Jersey, specialized in this type. Seventeen . . . but the kind of seventeen who had stopped reading the magazine by the same name at twelve.

She was blue eyed and beautiful. It was that sort of beauty helped a lot by great-looking clothes—a soft, black cashmere suit the same color as her straight, shoulder-length hair, and the kind of sophisticated makeup that looked natural until you realized eyes weren't outlined in black, lips weren't glossy, and cheekbones against olive skin did not have pink tones.

She was thin and tall. If she wasn't rich, she looked

it. She wasn't poor. Both her parents were Philadelphia shrinks who cost upward of one hundred dollars an hour.

"We didn't know him at all, apparently," said the doctor.

Just where his blazer buttoned, I could see the bulge of his potbelly, fighting the alligator belt holding it in. He was the blue-blazer (gold buttons), gray-flannel-pants type—Bean boots (the kind that lace), a storm coat (with a Burberry lining) tossed on my couch.

Lauren's coat was the female version of his, but her boots were high-heeled ones with fur tops.

"Fell," she said, "unless you have some definite information, you'd save Daddy a lot of agony by simply saying you know less than we do." She was one of those girls who called her father "Daddy," as my old girlfriend, Keats, always did. She treated him the same way Keats treated her father, as though there was no way he'd ever know as much about life as she did, but she was going to be patient with him just the same.

Girls like that can usually wrap Daddy around their little fingers when they want to. Me too.

I told them what she wanted to hear. "I know less than you do." I was glad to comply. I hadn't asked for this meeting. It was my only free period before lunch, then on to English class and the bad news probably awaiting me on my paper about Robert Browning. You don't think I understood "Fra Lippo Lippi," do you?

"No, no, no, no," Dr. Lasher said. "We came here to hear what you have to say, no matter how vague and uninformed. I'll listen to hunches at this point."

I told him my major reservation about Lasher's death being a suicide wasn't a hunch, exactly. My feeling was based on something my dad had told me about suicide: that a person who wore eyeglasses removed them before he jumped from a high place. He left them behind or put them in his pocket. I told him my father'd been a private detective, and a cop before that; it was just something he'd pointed out to me.

Lauren said, "My brother couldn't see his fingers in front of his face without his glasses. He'd have worn them."

"What else?" her father asked me.

I lied. "Nothing." The last thing I wanted was to get involved.

What I had to do was stay out of trouble that term. I'd been in enough last term to hold me for a lifetime, living up to my father's prediction that I'd head for trouble like a paper clip to a magnet: It was my nature.

I'd opened my mouth without thinking when I saw Lasher's body, and his broken glasses beside it. Someone had told Dr. Lasher what I'd said. Maybe even Dib, my best friend on The Hill. Dib had his own reasoning about Lasher's leap from the top of The Tower. Why had Lasher screamed? Does someone scream when he's planned to jump . . . or does he scream when he's *pushed*?

"What can you tell me about this fellow named Creery?" Dr. Lasher asked.

Winner, 1978 Christopher Award
Best Children's Books of 1978, *The New York Times*

Little Little
ALA Notable Children's Books of 1981
Best Books for Young Adults, 1981 (ALA)
Best Children's Books of 1981, *School Library Journal*
Winner, 1981 Golden Kite Award, Society of Children's Book Writers

What I Really Think of You
(A Charlotte Zolotow Book)
Best Children's Books of 1982, *School Library Journal*

Me Me Me Me Me: Not a Novel
(A Charlotte Zolotow Book)
Best Books for Young Adults, 1983 (ALA)

Him *She Loves?*
(A Charlotte Zolotow Book)

I Stay Near You
(A Charlotte Zolotow Book)
Best Books for Young Adults, 1985 (ALA)

Night Kites
(A Charlotte Zolotow Book)
Best Books for Young Adults, 1986 (ALA)
Recommended Book for Reluctant YA Readers, 1987 (ALA)

Fell
(A Charlotte Zolotow Book)
Best Books for Young Adults, 1987 (ALA)

Heavenly shades of night are falling—
it's Twilight Time.
Out of the mist your voice is calling—
it's Twilight Time . . .

Dib had decided Creery'd pushed Lasher. He'd overheard a fight between them just before Christmas vacation. During that fight Lasher had threatened to kill Creery. Dib had theorized Lasher'd tried to do it, and Creery had pushed him while he was defending himself.

Both Lasher and Creery were in The Tower that fatal afternoon.

Lauren jumped in to answer her father's question herself.

She said, "Cyril Creery is just a goofball." She laughed a little, as though there was something really cute about being just a goofball. "Cyr wouldn't harm a fly."

I noticed she was wearing a gold 7 around her neck. Only a member of the secret Sevens could buy one of those. I'd never heard of a Sevens giving one of those to his sister, not even Outerbridge, whose sister, Cynthia, looked like Madonna and sometimes came over from Bryn Mawr to be his date at dances.

Usually Sevens gave these things to their girlfriends, or their mothers, the same as Air Force men did with their wings.

I'd always known that Lasher had a thing about Lauren. He'd brought her name up any chance he could, and her photographs were all over his room.

Often, on weekends, Lasher'd disappear, telling us later he'd gone away with his sister. He'd never say where.

I was remembering that while Lauren sat there sighing, saying in a somewhat exasperated tone, "Cyril and Paul didn't like each other, that's for sure. But Cyril's no killer. Mon Dieu, Daddy."

I thought about someone blithely saying Mon Dieu, Daddy, dangling one great long stockinged leg over another while right that moment in chapel they were festooning the walls with black-and-white-striped mourning cloths for that afternoon's memorial service. Black for sorrow. White for hope. Her brother'd been buried only a few days ago.

"Fell?" said Dr. Lasher. "Is there anything you're not telling me?"

"If you've spoken to Dib, there isn't."

"To whom?"

"Sidney Dibble," said Lauren. "The one we took to breakfast."

I thought so.

"He knows what I know," I said.

Dr. Lasher said, "Tell me about Twilight Truth, Fell."

"We've gone all over that, Daddy."

"I want to hear Fell's version."

I said, "Damon Charles, The Sevens' founder, seemed to have a fondness for twilight. Sevens get married at twilight, and buried at twilight. No one knows why. . . . Then there's Twilight Truth, on the second Wednesday of the month. Any Sevens who feels honor bound to confess he's done something to make him unworthy of the privileges of Sevens leaves a written statement in the top of The Tower. The officer of the

day rings the tower bell and reads it over the bullhorn."

"And then?" the doctor asked.

"We come up with an appropriate penalty. If it's serious, we ask him to live and eat at the dorm, or we give him the silent treatment. . . . If it's not that serious, we suspend certain privileges. We whistle 'Twilight Time' in his presence. . . . Sometimes we whistle that to force Twilight Truth on him, if he doesn't seem likely to step forward on his own."

"So ridiculous!" said Lauren.

"It's just ritual," her father said. "All clubs, including sororities, have their rituals."

"Which is why I'd never join one!" she said.

The doctor passed me something Xeroxed.

"Have you seen this, Fell?"

I hadn't. It was signed by Cyril Creery.

CREERY: *That Wednesday afternoon Lasher said he left a copy of a letter I'd written up in The Tower. He said it would be read at Twilight Truth. We had a fight about it. I punched him. Then I took the elevator up, but of course there was no letter. He was going crazy—I knew that. We all did. . . . I took the elevator down and went into Deem Library in The Tower. . . . About ten minutes later he jumped from the top.*

LT. HATCH: *Did you think he'd made up a letter, or was there a real letter?*

CREERY: *My father had a stroke two years ago. Ever since, my stepbrother's been running our paint factory.*

Right before Christmas I wrote Lowell a letter. There was a lot of personal stuff in it. I was talking about changing my behavior and being more help to him.

I kept a copy. When Lasher mentioned a letter, naturally I thought of it. I was afraid he'd gone through my desk and found it. He wasn't above that sort of thing. . . . I wouldn't have wanted it read over a bullhorn. . . . So I went up to look, but he was bluffing.

LT. HATCH: *When you came back down and went into the library, who was there?*

CREERY: *No one was around that I could see. . . . I'd never kill anyone, not even Paul Lasher. I don't have it in me.*

Cyril Creery
Cottersville Police Report

I handed it back to Dr. Lasher.

"I didn't know about a letter," I said, "just that they had a fight."

"There wasn't a letter, apparently," said Lauren.

"It sounds like something Lasher'd do," I said. "They were always baiting each other. Lasher thought Creery was selling drugs. Lasher said you could get any kind of pill you wanted from him. He called his room 'The Drugstore.' "

Lauren said, "But Paul had become so paranoid! He

made up lies about everyone. Remember, Daddy? He said Mother hadn't asked him a personal question in five years."

"Both your mother and I neglected Paul."

"Oh, Daddy, I heard her with my own ears. How are you? How's school? How're things at Sevens?"

"Yes," said the doctor. "Very general questions. Hardly personal."

"What was she supposed to say?" said Lauren.

Her father answered, "We both should have said, 'Sit down, Paul. Tell us what's going on in your life.' "

"Stop blaming yourself, Daddy! *Please!*"

The noon bell rang.

"Fell has to eat now," said Lauren. "I'm hungry too. And Mother's waiting for us."

Maybe a death in the family didn't make Lauren lose her appetite. Mine was missing for weeks after my dad died. So was my mother's. My little sister's. As good a cook as I am, I couldn't even tempt them, and everything from my spaghetti carbonara to my Chinese chicken wings had tears in it.

Dr. Lasher didn't want to leave. "Your mother is with the headmaster," he said. "She's not waiting for us."

Lauren was already putting her long arms down the sleeves of her Burberry.

"What do you know about Rinaldo Velez?" Dr. Lasher asked me.

"Not much. He works in The Tower, waits table and stuff."

Lauren said, "My brother gave *him* the VCR and the

Mont Blanc pen. We think he might have given him his good Gstaad watch, too."

Was there such a thing as a bad Gstaad watch?

"Why?" I said.

I meant why Rinaldo of all people? He was a townie. He'd be someone who'd really value those gifts, of anyone on The Hill—someone unlikely to be able to afford anything like them; but Lasher hadn't ever had a reputation for being friendly, charitable, or even thoughtful. He'd called Rinaldo *"Flaco"* because of how skinny he was. *Flaco,* Lasher'd say, you know I don't eat beef—take this back. *Flaco,* he'd say, this spoon has soap film on it—get me another.

Lauren didn't get my drift. "My brother gave them to him because my brother was preparing to leave this life."

"No," was all Dr. Lasher said.

He didn't say it loudly.

Softly, he said it.

But he did say it emphatically, as though there was no possibility that Lasher was preparing to leave this life.

I felt the same way he did. No . . . no way.

2

TRY READING "Fra Lippo Lippi" and see if you understand it.

This poem by Browning, I'd written on my test paper, *tells a rather disgusting story about the famous martyr St. Laurence, and about the painting Fra Lippo Lippi did of him roasting on a gridiron in 258 A.D.*

After my father became a private detective, my mother started calling him "The Martyr" because of all the hard work he put in on the job.

But my father couldn't hold a candle to St. Laurence, famous for telling the men who had him on a spit over hot coals, "One side is done; now you can do the other side."

The only thing I could really remember the day of the test on Browning's poetry was this fellow getting off that zinger while the Romans were cooking him.

I didn't understand the poem.

John Fell, you don't understand this poem, Mr. Wakoski wrote in red ink across my paper. *It is not about St. Laurence. It's about the monk who painted him. You make it sound as though Fra Lippo Lippi was being roasted. Painting while he sizzled. Neat trick. Reread this poem. It is also a defense of artistic realism. . . . What's wrong with you, Fell? It's not a hard poem, no more so than "Andrea del Sarto."*

Einstein's theory of relativity might not be any harder

than Newton's law of gravity either, but you'd never prove it by me.

I was standing in the hall between classes reading Wakoski's remarks with a sinking heart, the D– at the top of my paper making my stomach turn over.

"Another A+?" Dib asked me.

"Look again," I said. He was already glancing down over my shoulder. He let out a surprised whistle and tried pushing back his blond hair from his eyes.

I'd roomed with him before I became a Sevens. We were both blonds, but there the resemblance ended. He was taller and younger and he lived on junk food, proving that metabolism may have more to do with weight than calories, because Dib was almost a skeleton. If I ate all the Hostess Ding Dongs and Drake's golden creme cups he put away in an afternoon, I'd be ten pounds heavier.

"Browning is hard." Dib tried to make me feel better.

We started walking along together. I hadn't seen him in almost a week. When I first got into Sevens and he didn't, I made a point of looking him up at the dorm nearly every day, to try and let him know things weren't going to be any different.

But things *were*. Once a Hill boy made Sevens, the others treated us differently . . . and I guess we contributed to the change too, because we were on our honor never to tell the secrets of Sevens, and never, never to let anyone know how we got into the club.

That was the big mystery: How did someone get invited to join Sevens?

I wished I could tell Dib. He would have howled. He was right beside me our first day of school, when all of us had to plant little evergreen trees. That was the first thing you did when you arrived at Gardner School: You got into a line with other new kids, and all of you planted your tree . . . and named it something. . . . Anything. . . . I remember Dib named his after his dog: Thor.

I named mine "Good-bye," on a whim. My old girlfriend, Keats, lived in a house called Adieu. I'd tease her about the French, tell her it was pretentious. What's wrong with plain old good-bye? I'd ask her. . . . It was good enough for me. Good-bye to her, and to Long Island where I'd met her. Good-bye to public high school. Hello to Pennsylvania and preppydom!

Nobody but a member of Sevens knows that what you name your tree is the most important thing you do at Gardner School. If you name it something with seven letters in it, you are automatically a Sevens member.

There's no more to it than that. No one ever makes the connection. Everyone thinks you've done something special, or are someone special, to get asked to join, but it's a fluke. Mere chance, as The Sevens like to sing. And from the moment you are initiated into Sevens, you live in the luxurious Sevens House, and eat in the Sevens clubhouse at the bottom of The Tower. . . . You get a lot more privileges, too. . . . The other kids resent you, and envy you . . . and like Dib, they can't believe you won't even give them a clue about how you got to be a privileged character overnight.

Dib continued talking about Browning. "The only line he wrote that I ever understood," he said, "is: *Grow old along with me! The best is yet to be.* And I'm not sure I agree with him on that point, either."

"Why don't you think the best is yet to be?"

"Because someone's getting away with murder," he said, "and I don't think anyone gives a damn!"

"You had breakfast with the Lashers. He seems to give a damn."

"He's the only one."

"Are you going to the memorial service?" I was trying to change the subject, I admit. Five more months and I'd be graduated.

"Yeah, I'm going," said Dib. "Shall I save you a seat?"

"I have to sit with The Sevens."

"Sorry I asked." He took a box of Old Crows from his pocket and offered me one.

"Didn't you just eat lunch?"

He popped a couple of the licorice candies into his mouth. "Why don't you want to talk about this, Fell? Did The Sevens say you can't discuss it?"

"Come on, Dib. It's not like that. I'm just trying to keep my nose clean this semester so I can get out of this place."

"But you were the one who started me thinking it wasn't suicide. *You* told *me* the thing about the smashed glasses."

"I wish I never had."

"But you did, Fell. And I told the Lashers."

"Did you tell them he was screaming?"

"I couldn't bring myself to."

"We should have, I suppose. Nothing seemed to faze Lauren. Her eyes glaze over if you even suggest it might not have been suicide. The case is closed where she's concerned."

"And she let Rinaldo keep everything Lasher gave him."

The class bell rang. I was due down the hall for Latin.

Dib said, "The VCR, the pen, et cetera! He got a lot of stuff from Lasher. He's even selling some of it. I wish I could afford the word processor."

"What kind of a word processor is it?" I needed one myself. "Maybe we could go in on it together."

"A Smith-Corona," Dib said. He grimaced and shook his head. "I feel like a vulture. . . . Maybe if I was trying a little harder to find out what exactly happened that day in The Tower, I wouldn't."

"All *right*!" I said. "Can you come to my room tonight, after dinner? We'll talk about it."

Everyone around us was disappearing into classrooms.

"You mean your suite, don't you?" Dib gave one of his sarcastic laughs. "Yeah, I'll come over about eight."

"Eight thirty," I said. "We eat our dinner slower at Sevens. You know how it is: You savor every morsel when you're eating roast turkey with stuffing . . . and mashed potatoes . . . and giblet gravy."

I decided to rub it in. At Main Dining they'd get something like chili over baked potato. He'd succeeded in making me feel guilty about Lasher's so-called suicide, but he wasn't going to do a number on me with The Sevens.

"Do they have doggie bags over there?" Dib said. "I wouldn't mind a turkey leg."

Second bell.

Then the carillon from chapel, playing "Farewell, old friend, farewell. Rest now, rest."

3

I miss you, Mom. Try not to (1) go shopping; (2) open any new charge accounts; (3) worry about me—I'm fine.

I stopped at the end of the letter and crossed out 1, 2, and 3. My mother didn't have a sense of humor about being a spendthrift. She'd take it as criticism. Trying to point anything out to her, such as the fact that every time she used a credit card she was borrowing money at around 19 percent interest, only made her mad. . . . I decided she was as entitled to her mistakes as I was to mine, even though I'd probably end up paying for my kid sister's college one day, at the rate Mom was dancing through Macy's, Bloomingdale's, Savemart, and Sears.

Don't worry about me. Give Jazzy a big kiss.

Love,

Johnny

P.S. I've ordered you something for your birthday.

Her birthday was at the end of February. She was a Pisces. She liked to remind everyone she was born the same day as Elizabeth Taylor . . . another great shopper.

I didn't know where I was going to get $175, but I'd checked *Gold 7, with necklace* on a Sevens order form and given it to Rinaldo. . . . In a week it would be delivered to my room, gift wrapped in the special 7's paper.

Although Mom liked to razz me about being in Sevens, I had an idea she was secretly impressed. We didn't have a lot going on in our life that singled us out from millions of other families who spent too much time watching the boob tube, using credit cards, and reading the gossip about people who went to Paris on the Concorde to have breakfast.

I'd gone over to The Sevens clubhouse before the memorial service to write the letter.

A lot of Sevens did their letter writing there, not just because there was always a fire on cold days in Deem Library and it was quiet, but also because the Sevens stationery was there. It was not supposed to be taken from that room. It was watermarked, cream-colored paper with THE SEVENS in light blue across the top. The stamps on the table were free. There were Parker pens with 7 on them in gold, the old-fashioned kind that took real ink. When you were finished, you just put your letters in the light-blue box marked CORRESPONDENCE, and the help got it to the post office.

There were always vases filled with fresh flowers in the library, even in January, and apple or cranberry juice in carafes on the table outside the door.

These little extras were just another reminder that we were special and privileged. Spoiled, my mom said, and you did nothing to deserve it. But that's what I liked about it. How could I feel guilty about things like having fresh sheets every day, and a maid to clean my room, when it all came about by mere chance?

I put my boots back on and got ready to walk down to chapel. It was snowing again, a wet one now, not the kind that sticks—and I walked along thinking about this girl I still loved—how she was out of my life without ever having been in it. I tried to picture her in winter clothes.

My relationships with females are a lot like the snow I was walking in, not the kind that stick.

There'd been Keats, who actually stood me up on the night of her prom, and that was just for starters . . . and then there'd been Delia.

My memories of Delia could melt the snow and turn the winter day into a July night with an orange ball up in the sky, a thousand stars, and the scent of roses, and I could even hear the sounds of that old Billy Joel song we danced to . . . but I wouldn't let myself go back.

Forget Delia, I told myself, and I almost laughed when Kidder gave my arm a punch down near chapel. "Fell?"

he said. "Come down from outer space. We need you here on earth. You were just light-years away. What were you thinking about? You walked right past me."

"I was just reviewing the quantum theory," I said, "relating it to blackbody radiation, relativity, and the uncertainty principle." Kidder didn't laugh at my joke.

"You know what I've been thinking about? How much I'm going to miss Lasher around the poker table. Did you ever play with him?"

"I couldn't afford it."

"Yeah, who could?" (Kidder could.) "He was good at cards, anyway."

Kidder had named his tree Key West, where his own little yacht was berthed. He could have been a model for Colgate toothpaste or jockey shorts, if he'd needed the money. He didn't.

We were both wearing our black-and-white-striped mourning bands on our overcoat sleeves. On our heads sat the black top hats Sevens wore outside of the clubhouse only for funerals.

"Look over there," said Kidder, nudging me, nodding toward a black Mercedes with MD license plates. It was stopped in front of the chapel, and I could see Lauren Lasher getting out of it, then her father.

But I think Kidder was calling my attention to the woman already standing on the curb. She was wrapped in mink from shoulders to ankles, sucking one last drag from a cigarette. A tall lady with black hair, black shades, and a face you'd pass on the street, then whirl around to see again.

I suddenly remembered Lasher's face when he wasn't wearing his glasses. He'd had a certain beauty too, broken and bloody last I'd seen it . . . as though he'd landed on the icy pavement headfirst.

Inside, the organist was playing "Just a Song at Twilight" like a dirge. There were red roses everywhere, including one across everyone's hymnal.

We put them in our lapels.

After all the guests had filed in, the organist stopped playing. The Sevens Sextet stood in front of their chairs on the platform, their top hats over their hearts. They sang a cappella the song played all afternoon on the carillon:

"Farewell, old friend, farewell.
Rest now, rest.
You did your best.
Farewell, dear heart, farewell.
Sleep now, sleep.
Your love we keep."

I tried to think of worse things than Lasher dying, which should have been easy since I'd never liked him. I pictured droughts in Africa, and the war-torn Middle East. Still, there were tears right behind my eyes. My mother was the same way at weddings, and whenever bands marched in parades. The floodgates opened.

Next it was Dr. Skinner's turn. He was Gardner's

headmaster, a big, bald, roly-poly fellow who always wore a vest so his Phi Beta Kappa key would show.

He was the eulogist.

Finding words to praise Paul Lasher was a challenge to anyone who hadn't played cards with him, but Skinner came up with some. They were mild enough for all of us to keep straight faces. He didn't pour it on. Sevens were always called by their last names, so he stood there fondling his gold key and said Lasher was always a presence on The Hill. He said Lasher loved this place, more perhaps than anyone he'd ever known. He said Lasher was a loyal member of Sevens. He said the song that would be sung next always meant a great deal to Lasher.

Outerbridge appeared then. When he sang his Sunday-morning solos, you were tempted to turn around and see if he was in a dress, his soprano was so high and tremulous. But now he was up in front, the single red rose in one hand, the top hat in the other, across his chest.

He sang the school song.

"Others will fill our places,
Dressed in the old light blue,
We'll recollect our races.
We'll to the flag be true.
And youth will still be in our faces
When we cheer for a Gardner crew.
Yes, youth will still be in our faces,
We'll remain to Gardner true."

I looked around the chapel. All dry eyes except for Lauren and her father. At least I think Lauren was crying. She had a handkerchief to her eyes. The lady in mink wore the black shades, but she didn't seem to be weeping, though her chin was stuck forward in the gesture of someone steeling herself.

Creery was the only Sevens not present. He had spent two nights in the infirmary. There were rumors he couldn't sleep, and others that he slept around the clock. It could be either way with Creery—he was famous for his changing moods. We'd heard that his stepbrother had been summoned from Florida, that Creery was threatening to leave Gardner.

I had last seen him the night of Lasher's death, at the assembly Skinner'd called us to, warning us not to discuss "this accident" with outsiders. He looked like the same old Creery to me: eyes that said no one's home, no one's expected.

As far as I knew, not one soul had signed up to speak at this memorial. The night before, I'd seen the sheet hanging on the Sevens bulletin board, still not a name on it.

I wasn't surprised, then, when Dr. Skinner said a member of the family, Dr. Inge Lasher, would say a few words.

She had the long black mink coat draped over her shoulders, the dark glasses pushed up on her head. She had the kind of eyes you'd think a shrink would have: radar ones, sending out as much as they took in, searching all our faces. They were as dark as brown could get.

The thick German accent was a surprise.

When she said we, it sounded like v. All her v's were w's, her w's v's. There were other things too. *She* vould haf said dere vere udder tings. That's just to give you an example.

Her very short speech turned out to be a minilecture on a new view of adolescent suicide. According to Inge Lasher, her son had a chemical abnormality in his brain.

It has been proven, said she, that young people who suffer from major depression, and attempt suicide or dwell on suicidal plans, secrete less growth hormone than other depressed but nonsuicidal young people or other healthy youngsters.

No one, she insisted, was responsible, or should feel guilt.

All her speech did for me was make me remember the scream. I'd never heard a scream like it. Not even in the worst splatter films. It was so unlike any everyday human sound, I hadn't known what it was until I'd seen him, what was left of him, crumpled there on the ice.

See what happens when you don't secrete enough growth hormone?

I couldn't buy it.

After she sat down, and before we Sevens gathered at the front to sing our song, Dr. Skinner made an announcement that caused a ripple through the chapel, all heads turning toward the rear when he was finished.

"And now, someone else who knew Lasher would

like to read something. Rinaldo Velez. . . . Would you come forward, please, Rinaldo?"

Rinaldo was The Tower jester. Although he had no accent, he affected one when he felt like it, sometimes peppering his conversation with Spanish words like *pijos* (yuppies) and *fachas* (fascists—said, with a grin, of The Sevens). He tried to teach certain Sevens *salsa sensual*, the song-and-dance craze he was master of, but he claimed we had *blanco* hips that didn't swivel, and our hearts weren't beating hot enough inside our bodies.

All last semester he'd belted out *"Ven Devorame Otra Vez"* from the kitchen: *"Come and Devour Me Again."*

He *was* skinny, and very tall, with silky black hair he slicked back and wore in a short cut.

Although he was a townie, Rinaldo sometimes had a proprietary feeling about Sevens. He stood behind me once in the dining room when we sang "The Star-Spangled Banner" on Veterans' Day. I'd forgotten the Sevens habit of placing your hand over your heart when you came to the words "at the twilight's last gleaming." Rinaldo reached around and put my arm up across my chest. I glanced over my shoulder at him and he gave me a stern look, the kind a parent would give a thoughtless child.

Had I ever seen him with Lasher anyplace but in the dining room, waiting on him? If I had, I didn't remember it.

Had anyone? Had anyone in Sevens even been asked what their connection was?

◻

I had never seen Rinaldo when he wasn't wearing a white waiter's jacket and a black clip-on tie. I had never seen him look so uncomfortable, either.

There was already perspiration dotting his forehead, where a lick of black hair dangled. His tight, black, two-buttoned double-breasted suit had wide shoulders with the waist nipped. He wore a black mock turtleneck.

His hands were shaking. He tried holding up the piece of paper he carried, but he could not read it until he'd flattened it on the top of the podium. Then he had to lean over and bend down his head.

His voice carried well, though it quivered and slipped out of its register a few times into a higher one, which made him pause and clear his throat.

No one could doubt that he had written the strange poem himself, though he had nothing to say in the way of introduction.

He just read.

> *"Here, he said, these are all for you.*
> *I have to leave.*
> *And it is true*
> *That I did not perceive,*
> *The circumstance . . .*
> *A backward glance,*
> *Then* Hasta la vista, *he said,*
> *And he was gone.*
> *And he is dead.*

"Here, he said, these are all for you.

"Here, this is my good-bye,
And that is all.
I never really knew you, Paul.
But here, let me say so long,
Before the Sevens song."

I got up then, along with the other Sevens, and we went to the front of the chapel.

Once again I felt slightly choked up. It had to be something about Rinaldo's poem . . . or maybe just that it was sad someone who hardly knew Lasher was the only one of us to come forward to say good-bye. Not even someone from The Hill. . . . And Rinaldo was probably shamed into doing it because Lasher'd given him stuff.

We sang with feeling; the words rang out. Maybe we were all thinking of the same thing: the way Lasher belted out those words:

. . . my heart will thrill
At the thought of The Hill
And the Sevens . . .

like a Marine singing "from the halls of Montezuma," like some newly freed hostage joining in on "God Bless America."

There was a brief silence at the end of our song.

Then, in unison, we said the Sevens farewell. From Tennyson.

"Twilight . . . and evening bell . . .
And after that . . . the dark."

The chapel bell tolled seven times.

4

LAUREN SAW ME outside the chapel, waved, and beckoned me with her finger.

The campus lights were on. We stood in the cold wet rain that had turned most of the snow to slush. I felt foolish in my top hat; it'd always been a bit too big.

She was carrying her red rose. Over by their Mercedes, I saw Dr. Skinner helping her mother into the front seat.

Her gloved hand held an umbrella over her head. On the other hand, long nails, unpainted but glossy. A ring with a red stone.

"I'll come back to pack Paul's things next week, or the week after," she said. "Does it matter?"

"You know, I'm fairly new here," I told her. "I'm not the one to ask."

"Then why do you act as though you're in charge?"

I hadn't expected that, nor her sharp tone.

"I don't. Why do you think I do?"

"You're the one with all the opinions."

"You came to me and asked for them," I reminded her.

"*I* didn't. I came with Daddy."

She was toying with the gold 7 around her neck, under her Burberry. She went right on. "We're going to give Rinaldo my brother's clothes. Apparently that's who Paul wanted his things to go to. . . . And he can keep everything Paul gave him."

"Why tell me?" I asked her.

"So you don't start any rumors about that, too."

"I didn't start any rumors, Lauren. I made a comment to Dib."

"Which was overheard by a lot of people."

"I blurted it out. I wasn't trying to spread it around."

"I wish you'd tell Cyr you were the one. He thinks it was Rinaldo."

"Why does he care? No one said *he* did it." Not out loud, anyway.

"We don't want all these rumors and bad feelings between you guys. Just let Paul rest in peace."

"Gladly," I said, "but why does Creery care?"

"Because of that fight they had. How would you feel if someone jumped to his death immediately after you'd had a fight with him?"

"They were always fighting, Lauren."

"Still."

"Don't worry about Creery. He'll roll a few joints and forget all about it."

"He claims there's such a thing as The Sevens Revenge."

"That's an old rumor. . . . Besides, what did he do to deserve The Revenge?"

I'd heard of it, of course. It was said that if you told The Sevens secrets, or if you were guilty of Conduct Unforgivable, you were taken to The Tower and a live rat was tied around your neck. Surviving that, you were given the silent treatment until you resigned and left Gardner. There were other versions, each with a rat in it . . . and though The Revenge supposedly had not been performed since 1963, rumors about it were part of Sevens lore. One death was attributed to The Revenge. An automobile accident an alumnus had, while a rat was tied to his ankle, was said to be The Revenge too.

I tried a smile, to lighten things up. I smelled her perfume and thought I knew its name. Obsession. Keats always wore it. Lauren didn't smile back at me. I was getting wet. She made no attempt to share the umbrella.

She said, "*Latet anguis in herba.* Do you know your Latin?"

"I know that Latin. Your brother taught it to me."

She decided to translate it anyway. "The snake hides in the grass."

"It was his motto," I said.

"Sometimes I can see why it was," she said. "Fell, I

don't happen to believe in hormonal loss. What I believe is that people who don't know how to care about other people get obsessed with things. Clubs, for example. The way my brother was about Sevens."

I didn't know what she was leading up to, but I couldn't have agreed more. I was always suspicious of guys who got too attached to their schools or their private clubs and fraternities. I figured they were probably getting their first taste of belonging anywhere, that maybe no one had ever made them feel important before.

"I know," I said. "Your brother felt about Sevens the way a Doberman feels about his backyard."

"I don't think it did Paul any good. A club doesn't love back. It can't take the place of people. You get twisted putting all your energy into a club."

"I think so too," I said. I was a little amazed that we could agree on something.

Then she said, "A theory *theories*, do the same thing when you begin to put all your energy into them."

She wasn't talking about Lasher and Sevens anymore. She was after me.

"People with too many theories about other people don't have real feelings for other people," she said.

"I have both," I told her. I was getting wetter. "If I was carrying that umbrella, you'd be under it, along with all my theories."

"Touché," she said. "Get under for a sec."

While I did, she said, "What I'm going to ask you to do isn't my idea—it's Daddy's. And you might as well know Dr. Skinner said you weren't the ideal person to ask."

"Well? Ask."

"You have too much attitude, Fell."

"I was thinking that about *you* this morning."

"My brother did a lot of writing. Daddy wants to take his best pieces and put them in a memorial book. Would you read through everything and select them?"

"Why does Daddy think I'm the one to do that, and Skinner think I'm not?"

"Daddy likes you. Skinner thinks you're better off not dwelling on Paul's death."

I was too curious to play hard to get, and the wind was pushing the rain down my neck.

Lauren said, "Daddy will pay you, of course."

"All right. I'll give it a try. Where are the manuscripts?"

"They're with Mrs. Violet at Sevens House. Your name is on the package."

"You and Daddy aren't short on confidence."

"Dr. Skinner said *you* were short on cash, so you'd have to get a hundred dollars, at least. Daddy thought that was cheap."

"I have to get a new business manager. Skinner's not working out at all."

Down by the black Mercedes, Lauren's father called out, "Come on, honey!"

She said, "One other thing: Daddy wants a few pictures of Paul in the memorial book. I'm going through his album, and I'll get some to you."

"Does your father know your brother wrote a lot about death and suicide?"

"Paul used to keep a noose in his room. He'd tell mother it was just in case he felt like having a last swing. . . . We were used to Paul."

Lauren's father called her again.

She said, "But now both my parents are into denial." Inside the Mercedes her mother honked the horn impatiently, three times.

5

THE SEVENS had turkey roast on Friday nights, steak on Wednesdays. Always fresh vegetables, fresh asparagus that night. Don't ask me where they managed to find it the last week of January.

While we ate, the committee for The Charles Dance was announced, and I was on it.

Named for The Sevens' founder, it was a major event at Gardner, held every March on our anniversary. Dorm boys and their dates were invited too. Females wore evening dresses, but all males came in costume as someone named Charles. The ill-omened rulers of England and France were favorites, from Charles II (the Fat) to Charles III (the Simple), but any Charles would do.

In the dining room of The Tower the only art was a lighted portrait labeled *Wife of Damon Charles*. We knew that if Gardner ever went coed, as our trustees were threatening, female Sevens would be outraged that like Lot's wife in the Bible, she had no name of her own. Did The Sevens even know what it was? I doubted it. She was a handsome and regal brunette in a white gown and pearls. Underneath *Wife of Damon Charles* was a quote from Wordsworth:

Her eyes as stars of twilight fair;
Like twilight's, too, her dusky hair.

Before the chocolate cake was served, while the uniformed waiters cleared the table under the candlelit chandelier, we all sang our song together.

"When I was a beggar boy,
And lived in a cellar damp,
I had not a friend or a toy,
But that was all changed by mere chance!
Once I could not sleep in the cold,
And patches they covered my pants,
Now I have bags full of gold,
For that was all changed by mere chance!
Mere chance, mere chance."

Rinaldo made an entrance from the kitchen, carrying a tray filled with cake on the light-blue 7's-crested plates.

"Mere chance makes us gay,
Mere chance makes night day,
But whoever she'll choose,
She can also make lose.
Mere chance has her way,
Mere chance."

I leaned back in my chair to try and get his attention. I wanted to say I'd see him after dinner. If I didn't move fast on that word processor, someone else would. Maybe now that he'd become heir to so many valuables, he'd let Dib and me pay in installments. Maybe not . . . and maybe he'd charge too much. But I ought to get it settled.

He went right past me, looking straight ahead, ignoring my *"Pssst!"* There was a watch on his wrist, lots of gold and stainless steel. The good Gstaad?

I decided to take a look at his shoes. My dad used to tell me a man's shoes say a lot about him. That was back before everyone was into Reeboks, when shoeshine still meant eager/accountable/ready.

And sure enough, Rinaldo had on black Reeboks.

Suddenly I saw very clearly one white Reebok get between Rinaldo's black ones.

Next, Rinaldo was on the floor.

So was the silver tray and the cake and the china.

The white Reebok had disappeared under the table.

I took a look at its owner. I never had liked that face. It used to remind me of my own, back when I was running with fast-track kids in Brooklyn, rebelling against being a cop's son, proving I could get as wrecked as anyone else.

Out of the infirmary, Creery seemed fully recovered. A skinhead last semester, he was letting his hair grow in. He already had a thin tail in back, reaching down toward his neck. There were the same two skull earrings in his right ear, and a silver GUNS N ROSES pendant around his throat.

At the sound of Rinaldo and the cake plates crashing to the floor, Creery's mouth twitched almost imperceptibly. He did not look over his shoulder to see the damage he had caused.

Since Lasher's death it hadn't been fear of seeing my old self in that face. It was more the feeling that if I did take a good look at it, I'd see Lasher in those eyes of Cyril Creery's. I'd see Lasher

f
a
l
l
i
n
g . . . the way a certain old girlfriend of mine—Delia—always used to write my name:

F
E
L
L

"DID ANYONE ELSE see Creery trip him?" Dib asked.

"I doubt it. I was the only one looking at Rinaldo's feet."

"Then what happened?"

"Rinaldo picked himself up. He and the other waiters cleaned up the mess, and they brought out more cake. You know The Sevens: The good life always goes right on."

"I don't know The Sevens," said Dib. "I only know you."

"You know what I mean, though. If there's a soul mourning for Lasher, I don't know who that'd be."

Dib was tearing the wrapper from a Milky Way. "How does somebody get into Sevens when no one even likes him?"

I let the question hang there.

Dib said, "Got any instant coffee?"

"Help yourself."

I didn't live in a room—Dib was right when he said that earlier in the day. I lived in a suite. Dib got off the bed and went into the other room, where there was a small refrigerator, a hot plate, a leather couch, a coffee table, some chairs, and a view of The Tower from the window. Private bath on the right.

I stretched out while I listened to an old Talking Heads

song and thought about the reason Creery would be gunning for Rinaldo. Because of what Lauren had told me, I supposed. Because Creery thought Rinaldo'd spread the rumor Lasher'd been murdered.

If someone had spread a rumor about me being a kleptomaniac, I wouldn't react unless I'd had a habit of walking out of stores with things hidden in my pockets.

Creery had always looked for a fight with Lasher. He was our resident cynic. He'd named his tree Up Yours. He'd slap his knee and laugh hysterically when Lasher'd speak about Sevens in the same way someone in a cult would drool over their guru. I remember how he cracked up once when Lasher had explained the habit old grads had of meeting for drinks only at hotels and restaurants with seven letters in the names. The Ritz, in Boston. Laurent, in New York. Creery'd almost wet his pants over that one.

Lasher had hated him, too. Everyone in the Sevens House was familiar with the scent of incense wafting from Creery's room, masking the marijuana smell inside. He was not the only pot smoker on The Hill, or in Sevens, but he was the only one who took advantage of the freedom we enjoyed in Sevens House, where there were no proctors or faculty, and Mrs. Violet, our housemother, rarely came above the first floor.

He flouted our self-regulatory system flagrantly. There was always one. Some grumbled about it; most minded their own business.

It was the kind of thing Lasher would lose sleep over.

He'd dog Creery's footsteps, whistling "Twilight Time" and promising to get Creery.

Lasher'd been in Sevens since he was fourteen.

Lasher used to get tears in his eyes when he'd hear the song The Sevens sing to let guys know they're in. The one we sang at the memorial service. Creery'd ride him about it, put his knuckles to his eyelids and mimic him.

I didn't know much about Lasher's life before he got to The Hill, but he'd named his tree Suicide.

Even after he was in the club, he wrote all these plays about Death, and he kept a noose in his suite at Sevens, too. Creery always asked him why he was stalling, why didn't he pee or get off the pot.

Still, it didn't seem like old cool-head Creery to care whether or not there were rumors Lasher'd been murdered. Unless he'd had something to do with the murder.

Dib came back with some Taster's Choice, turned down Talking Heads, and asked me point-blank if I thought Creery was capable of murder.

"My dad used to say anyone's capable of it, but not many are sufficiently provoked at the same time they have a weapon handy. That's why he was against ordinary people having guns around."

"What about being sufficiently provoked by someone while you're at the edge of a cliff . . . or standing on top of that tower?"

"Same thing, I guess."

"What about defending yourself when someone's about to murder you . . . and there you are at the top of that tower?"

"It could have happened that way. . . . I remember the night I got in Sevens: Suddenly Lasher was right behind me at the top of that thing. He said, 'Look down there at the ground and tell me if it makes you want to jump.' "

"You never told me this." There was always a slightly resentful tone when Dib would discover I wasn't reporting back to him the way we used to tell each other everything, anything, before Sevens, when the two of us were new on The Hill.

"He was holding me near the edge of the wall, and I thought, He's crazy. I'm up here by myself with this maniac."

"What did you do, Fell?"

"There's an elevator in The Tower, you know."

"I didn't know."

"Not many people outside of Sevens do. Creery came out of it at that point and told Lasher to knock it off. . . . Lasher was just trying to scare the hell out of me. All of Sevens knew I was up there with him, but I didn't know they did."

"Fell," Dib said, "Creery killed Lasher. I'm positive of it."

That was when a new voice was added to the conversation. Lionel Schwartz's. You could have said he was the president of Sevens, except president had nine letters in it instead of seven. So Schwartz was our captain.

"Sidney Dibble," he said, "you've got a wild imagination." He was chuckling like a lenient parent who'd just heard his three-year-old say the F word.

We called him The Lion. He wanted to be an actor. He had on a tweed sport coat with leather elbow patches, a red bow tie against a blue-and-white-striped shirt. Dark-brown hair cut short and parted down the center. John Lennon spectacles. He always looked like a lot of planning went into how he looked.

The Lion was the kind of guy you didn't get next to easily. You saw him in all the school plays. You couldn't miss him strutting around campus while everyone called out his name and hoped he'd remember theirs. He had SPECIAL written all over him.

He was also the kind of guy Dib envied and resented. I would have too, if I hadn't made Sevens. But propinquity changes your view of people. In Sevens we knew his mother was a madwoman, in and out of institutions. We'd hear him trying to reason with her on the house phone, reassuring her that the doctor wasn't from the CIA, that the neighbors weren't making bombs, and telling her no, he couldn't come home, not in midterm.

We knew certain Sevens' deepest secrets, guarding them as if they were our own.

But to Dib Lionel Schwartz was arrogant and vain. Worse, he was patronizing. I could feel Dib losing ground facing him down. "There're a lot of unanswered questions," Dib muttered.

"There always are when someone kills himself." Schwartz was still smirking, rocking on his heels with his hands stuck in the pockets of his trousers. He told Dib, "I'd like to talk with Fell, if it's all right with you."

Dib jumped to his feet and said it was fine with him, he'd see me tomorrow.

"How long is the talk going to take?" I asked Schwartz. I figured Dib could sit it out downstairs in our reception room.

But Dib didn't wait for The Lion's answer.

"I've got a paper to write tonight anyway," he said.

He was out of there.

SCHWARTZ SAT DOWN in the captain's chair next to my bed.

"Seven," he said to me. So he was there on Sevens business, following the formalities. This ritual was to seal our conversation as confidential. Probably they did it at The Ritz and Laurent, too. Maybe someday years from then I'd be meeting someone, leaning on my cane, my hair white, starting off "Seven."

I came up with seven things that went together, as I was expected to do.

"Pride, Wrath, Envy, Lust, Gluttony, Avarice, Sloth," I said.

"The Seven Deadly Sins. So be it. . . . Fell, you're about to receive an honor."

"I *am*?"

"An old member is asking for our help, and you've been chosen for the assignment."

"I see," I said.

"Were you expecting the Croix de Guerre or something?" he asked. He laughed and swung his legs up on my bed.

"What kind of an assignment?"

"Tutoring. That's part of it."

"I just got a D– in English."

"That's a fluke, isn't it, Fell? After all, you won the New Boys Competition last fall for your essay, and you wrote a rather remarkable paper on Agamemnon's death. . . . Dr. Skinner reminded me of all that when I discussed this with him."

"I didn't know Skinner was told Sevens' business."

"He wasn't told very much about the assignment, but I wanted his recommendation because it takes you off campus."

"And he recommended me?"

"He said you could use the money, which amounts to six dollars an hour . . . and he thinks you may have overreacted to Lasher's death, that it would be good for you to be busy."

"Is that also why I'm on the committee for The Charles Dance?"

Schwartz smiled. "No. *I* chose you for that. You haven't been on any of our committees."

Lasher's manuscripts were in the envelope on my desk. As curious as I was, I hadn't had a chance to glance at them.

Dib was going to offer Rinaldo three hundred for the word processor, one fifty apiece. I needed money—Skinner was right. I wasn't sure I needed Skinner telling everyone I needed it.

"This assignment concerns a girl who lives right here in Cottersville," Schwartz began. "Her father's a benefactor of Gardner—a very generous one, particularly to Sevens. Her name is Nina Deem."

"As in Deem Library?"

"Exactly," said Schwartz. "It was donated by the Deem family."

"Does she go to school in Cottersville?"

"Yes. She's a junior at Cottersville High. She'd probably be over in Miss Tyler's, except two years ago her mother died. There aren't any other children. She's all David Deem has. . . . She's a good writer, wants to be a professional, plans to go to Kenyon College. They have a whole writing program there."

"You can't tutor someone in writing. You mean help her with her grammar and her spelling and stuff like that?"

"Help her get back to writing. She's lost interest."

"Because I don't know anything about grammar and spelling. I need help with that myself."

"I *said* help her get back to writing. . . . The hidden agenda is more important than the tutoring, anyway."

"What does that mean, the hidden agenda?"

"It means there's another part to the assignment."

He reached inside his sport coat and took out a photograph. He passed it across to me.

"Edward Dragon," he said.

Dragon looked about my age, seventeen. He had a certain clean, American-boy quality, the kind models for Ralph Lauren's clothes have when they're shown in ads riding around in the family jeep with Dad, Sis, and the dog. He wasn't in a jeep, though. The backdrop was almost comical, as though he'd posed for it at a carnival or a fair. Behind him was a fake waterfall, an old mill, and a weeping willow tree.

He was seated on a real bench in front: brown suit, white shirt, and maroon-and-white-striped tie. His hair was the same dark brown, short and straight, slicked back. He was holding a Siamese cat on his lap.

I started to hand it back to Schwartz.

"Keep it," he said. "You'll need to know that face."

"What does he have to do with Nina Deem?"

"I'm coming to that. Last summer Nina enrolled in a writers' workshop held at the Cottersville Community Center. Dragon did too. The Center isn't far from the Deems' house, and Dragon would walk her home nights after class. He told her he was from Doylestown, and that he was a freshman at Penn State. Told her he was nineteen, and told Mr. Deem he was premed. That really appealed to Deem. He never went to college, never had a profession. You know Sun and Surf?"

"The sporting goods store?"

"That's his."

"How'd he afford to give us a library then?"

"That store's a little gold mine, Fell! Apparently he's a genius when it comes to money. He started from scratch, right out of Gardner. Like a lot of men without a formal education, he's in awe of doctors, lawyers, et cetera. He thought Dragon was the perfect guy to escort his daughter around."

Schwartz took his legs off my bed, crossed them, and tipped back in the chair. "Deem really liked him too. He trusted him like a son. Nina was under a shrink's care since her mother's death, shutting herself off from the world, depressed, that sort of thing. Dragon got her out and about: tennis, swimming at the club, the movies. He was her first real boyfriend, too. So . . ." The Lion shrugged his shoulders.

"So they fell in love and were miserable ever after," I said.

Schwartz held up one hand. "Hold your horses, Fell. It's not really a love story, though she was certainly in love. Whatever *he* felt, he was lying to her. He wasn't going to Penn State at all. Then one night late last fall the Cottersville police arrested him. The age on his driver's license was twenty-three. . . . They picked him up for selling cocaine."

"Was she with him?"

"No. Fortunately. It was around midnight. He was in a bar down near the train tracks. It was in the papers. That's how David Deem heard about it. . . . Dragon had a smart lawyer, and supposedly it was a first offense. He got off. But Deem told him he was never to see Nina again." Schwartz looked at me. "That's where you come in, Fell. You keep an eye out for him."

"I'm supposed to go there under false pretenses?"

"What other kind of pretenses are there? . . . Didn't your father do something like this for a living?"

"He was a cop and he was a detective. This is different."

"Not that different," Schwartz said. "Fell, this is a Sevens assignment. It's not an unreasonable one. Deem has done a lot for us. Do you think we take and never give back?"

I just sat there.

"This is a nice girl," Schwartz said. "Suppose you had a sister and—"

"I have a sister." She wasn't in first grade yet.

"And suppose she was hanging out with some pusher who'd lied to her and your family?"

"My sister wouldn't hang out with a known pusher." I thought of the day my father'd told me the last thing he ever thought he'd find in his own son's bureau drawer was shit. When he wasn't making out reports and calling pot "a controlled substance," he called it what we did on the street. Shit. He said that was the name for it, all right. He said, What in the name of God are you doing with this, Johnny? . . . What made me so sure Jazzy'd be invulnerable?

Back to Schwartz. "Suppose she fell in love with someone like Dragon and couldn't help herself?"

"Is that the case with Nina Deem?"

"It seems to be. She's promised Deem she won't see Dragon again, but Deem's not taking any chances."

Then he said, "You've had all the benefits of Sevens without any responsibility, Fell. You haven't volunteered once for any service to Sevens."

I sat there. I hated pushers. . . . It wasn't that. It was going there as something I wasn't, suckering some girl into trusting me when all the while she couldn't if she tried to see this Dragon.

"You'll be making fifty dollars a week."

Tiny mind that I admit having, it went to Mom's birthday and the gold 7. It went to the word processor Dib and I were hoping to buy from Rinaldo.

"Mostly you'll be a tutor," Schwartz said. "She really wants help getting into Kenyon."

"Have you ever met her?"

"Once. She was a sweet kid. After her mother drowned, I was part of the group Sevens sent to the funeral. . . . Let me tell you something, Fell. I think this assignment will be good for you. I think you've overreacted to Lasher's death too." I started to say something, but he held his hand up again. "Wait. Listen. I think the Fates arrange exits and entrances for us. When I came to The Hill, we'd just committed my mother to someplace. She'd look out her window through bars, with people around her who cawed like crows. My dad was telling me just get on with my education, but I was going to have to do it on a shoestring, we were so broke because of what she'd cost us. I had a scholarship, but I didn't have a dime in my pocket. . . . I couldn't get her out of my head. I even named my tree after her, I was so guilty. . . . Her name is Mildred."

"Seven letters."

"Exactly. Exits and entrances, Fell. I have a feeling this is an entrance for you."

"Enter the two-faced tutor."

"You'll be helping her, Fell!"

"Her mother drowned?"

"In their pool. This poor kid needs rescuing."

Schwartz was getting up. He knew he'd made the assignment without my even telling him. He'd used all his big guns: his mother, my sister, rescuing some innocent female, what I owed Sevens, the extra money I'd make. He'd shot me down.

"Oh, and Fell? She's a jet crash now, thanks to Dragon. Don't bring up Lasher's suicide. She doesn't need to hear about that sort of thing. You ought to forget it, too."

He reached out and grabbed my hand. "A week from next Wednesday afternoon at four, Fell. Her address is outside on your coffee table. She's expecting you."

THE DAY THAT I WAS to go to the Deems' to meet Nina, two strangers showed up on The Hill.

One came early that morning, after breakfast. He was a grief counselor from Philadelphia, there to meet with any students still reacting to Lasher's suicide. He parked his car in the faculty lot and went to the student lounge, where he would be available all day.

His car was a red bi-turbo 425 Maserati, with HEADOC on the license plates.

"Where did they find him?" Dib asked me as we walked to lunch.

"He's a Sevens," I said. "Class of '74."

"That figures," Dib said.

The only meal The Sevens ate in the Gardner dining room was lunch. The other stranger was there, at Dr. Skinner's table. He was tanned from the Miami sun, so Miami in his appearance that he stood out like a cop at a bikers' rally. His face was too young for the mop of white hair, thick and silky, a lock falling across his forehead. He had a white mustache curved down around the corners of his mouth, where there was a cheerful smile with even white teeth, and dimples.

He must have come directly from the airport. White suit, brown silk shirt, red-and-tan-patterned silk tie. He looked like Florida's version of Mark Twain.

Dib passed me the word going around our table.

"He's Creery's stepbrother. Lowell something."

Creery was beside him, wearing his wraparound blue Gargoyle shades, shoveling down tuna melt while Skinner and Lowell something talked.

"They say Creery wants to go back to Florida with him," Dib said.

"Good!"

"Why is it good? Then the whole thing will be forgotten."

"We're not getting anywhere anyway."

"Because your heart isn't in it, Fell! Now you're going to tutor some townie, and that'll end it."

I couldn't tell Dib everything about the Sevens assignment, or even that it *was* an assignment. I'd told him Skinner'd put me on to the job, and Dib decided it was part of the school cover-up.

Dib said, "Even if somebody tells his suspicions to that grief counselor, you don't think a guy with HEADOC on his license plate is going to take it seriously?"

"Here's a joke for you, Dib," I said. "A guy comes into a therapist's office and he says, Doc, I'm a wigwam. No, I'm a teepee. . . . No, I'm a wigwam. No, I'm a teepee. . . . The therapist says to the guy, Relax, you're two tents."

"Very funny, Fell," Dib said. "About as funny as this tuna fish is fresh."

"The point is," I said, "you have to relax. You *are* too tense. We'll just keep our eyes and ears open. We can't do any more than that."

"You haven't even questioned Rinaldo to find out why Lasher'd choose him to give his stuff to."

"He's bringing the word processor to my room after lunch. I'll do it then."

"Make sure the tutorial's in it so we know how to work it."

"I keep it until April, right? Then it's yours."

"But I can practice on it in your room, okay?"

"Okay," I said.

Dib said, "They say Creery is afraid of The Sevens Revenge, Fell. Did you hear anything about that?"

"Of course not. I'd tell you if I had."

"I'm not so sure," said Dib. "Anyway . . . why would he be afraid if he didn't have anything to do with Lasher's death?"

"Good question, Dib. But The Sevens Revenge is a myth."

"Sure, Fell, just a myth."

⧈

While we were all eating lunch, Lauren Lasher had come by Sevens House and packed up her brother's things.

She'd left a note on my desk.

Rinaldo will pick up Paul's clothes. How are you coming with the memorial book? Here are two photos, but still looking for a smiling one.

LL

In one snapshot she'd left on my blotter, Lasher

looked more like Lauren than he looked like himself. It was a head shot of him in a parka. Without his glasses he was almost beautiful, with thick, coal-black hair and dark, solemn eyes.

In the other photo there was a girl posed beside him in a long evening gown. He was dressed up in aviator's clothes, goggles covering his eyes, "Lindy" stitched over his pocket. He must have been impersonating Charles Lindbergh at the last Charles Dance.

It had taken me a week to get through his manuscripts.

He reminded me of Jazzy during "the terrible twos." My father was working nights then on a warehouse theft case on the Brooklyn docks. He was sleeping in the daytime, or trying to. Jazzy was literally screaming for attention: throwing her food at the walls when we'd put it in front of her, dumping in her pants the minute we'd take her off the potty, anything to keep our attention focused on her. She missed playtime with Daddy.

Lasher was doing a number with Death. He had titles like "The Graveyard Calls My Name" and "Death Be My Lover." His writing had all the organization and lyricism of some little tone-deaf child seated at a piano. He banged and pounded, hit-and-miss.

The only one I liked was one he'd worked and reworked for English. I remembered it from Mr. Wakoski's class last term. It was a play about a heaven where you were ranked according to the age you died: the younger, the better for you. In Lasher's paradise the ones who'd lived to grand old ages were called "The Feebles" and denied wings. The top angels were small babies who'd survived only a day or two.

He'd called it "Only the Young Fly Good."

That one I'd pulled out for the memorial book—grim and ironic as it was, it had humor.

I fastened the photos to it with a paper clip and shoved them in the top drawer.

I had a free study period before I was due down at the Deems'. There was a Latin test coming up, and I got out Cicero and began working my way through one of his senate speeches.

At two o'clock Rinaldo came staggering into my room with the top half of the word processor.

"The typewriter's out in the hall, Fell."

I brought it in while Rinaldo set everything up for me.

"You're getting a bargain," he said. "If I had time to learn it, I'd keep it for myself."

"Have you tried it out?"

"How would I try it out when I don't know how it works? I just know how it's put together, from taking it apart when Lasher gave it to me."

I checked to be sure the tutorial was in it; then I asked Rinaldo, "When did you two become such good friends?"

He gave me an exasperated look. Under his duffel coat he had on his work clothes: the black pants, white shirt, black plastic bow tie.

"We weren't good friends, Fell, and everyone knows it. We weren't friends at all. Are you fishing, is that it?"

"That's it."

"Walk down the hall with me," he said. "I want to show you some things in Lasher's room."

I walked with him while he told me the arrangements he'd made with Dib to pay him for the Smith-Corona.

"If it was disc instead of tape, you'd have paid a lot more," he said. "That model's out-of-date now. Lasher had a new computer ordered."

"A Porsche, a new computer. Why would he—"

Rinaldo didn't let me finish. "I know what you're going to say. Lauren Lasher filled me in on all your theories. They're right up there with her mother's *mierda* about hormones causing suicide."

"*Lack* of hormones," I said.

"Either way."

We were in Lasher's room then.

"Look around this place," Rinaldo said.

There was one lone poster left on the wall: Uncle Sam pointing his finger as he did on recruitment billboards. Under him: *Join the Army. Visit strange and exotic places. Meet fascinating people. And kill them.*

There were dozens of cartons packed with books, marked for the Gardner Library. The closets were open and empty. In one corner there was a leather massager-recliner, which Rinaldo kicked gently with one foot. "This has a built-in AM/FM/cassette stereo player," he said. "It cost about two thousand dollars."

He pointed to a walnut pants presser by the window. "That's a Corby Pants Press," he said. "Around two hundred and fifty dollars. . . . Want to look in the bedroom a minute?"

"What's there?"

"A Lifecycle," he said. "It has a matrix of sixty-four light displays changing terrain as you ride. It gives you pedaling speed, elapsed time, and calories you're burning. Costs about one thousand five."

"What's your point, Rinaldo?"

"There's no mystery here, Fell," he said. "You wonder why he gave stuff to me. He felt like it. Who would he give it to? No one liked him. Compared to what he had, he gave me a few little peanuts. He did it on impulse, the same way he bought all this like he could buy his happiness. He *pissed* money away, Fell. His family's, his own."

I nodded. "I can see he did."

"Money didn't mean anything. He made a pile of it every weekend down on Playwicky Road, playing cards. You know he had an apartment there? Number six Playwicky. That's where he went weekends he didn't go home. Ask Kidder."

The apartment was news to me. I said, "I believe you."

"Finally they're believing Rinaldo." He moved over to the couch and began sorting through jackets and pants piled there. "I told Creery's stepbrother: *Listen!* Rinaldo does not know zilch about any letter. *Nada!* . . . Look at these clothes, Fell. Where am I going to wear stuff of this kind? Am I going to strut around at a dance looking like some *blanco* preppy? You want to buy anything here?"

"I have to pay you for the word processor, remember?" I said. "Is that what's bothering Creery? He thinks you have the copy of the letter he wrote?"

"He thinks. His stepbrother thinks. But not anymore. I set them straight this morning. *Hola,* look at this suit, Fell! All this good cashmere and it's cut like a tent!"

"Rinaldo, why do they think *you've* got the copy of the letter?"

"They *thought*. They don't think it now. . . . Because he gave me his things, they thought he gave me his confidences. You ask me, nobody got those."

"Did you hear the fight between Creery and Lasher?"

"All the way in the kitchen! Sure! Lasher said he had the letter and Creery said, Were you going through my things? *Sweat* it, Lasher shouts, and he tries to whistle 'Twilight Time.' Then *POW!* I heard the smack Creery gave him too. But they were always at it!"

"Who was in The Tower that afternoon?"

"You think I know? I *said* I was in the kitchen. Most of The Sevens had classes, gym. . . . You sure you don't want to buy something here, Fell? I'll give you credit."

"I don't want to wear his clothes," I said. "You wear somebody's clothes, you get their luck, too."

"I never heard that," Rinaldo said. I wasn't surprised, since I'd just made it up. "Only thing I heard is you give someone shoes, they walk away from you."

He laughed and gave my shoulder a punch. "I gave a girl some of those stilt-heel pumps with no toes? She danced out of my life like a tornado leaving a Kansas barn on the ground in little pieces."

I said, "One danced out of my life the same way, and I hadn't given her anything."

"Maybe that's why," said Rinaldo.

We shut the door behind us, and I went back to put Cicero away and get into my boots and coat.

I checked a Cottersville map to see where Jericho Road was and to figure out my bus route to the Deems'.

I noticed that Playwicky was two streets down from where I was going.

THE DEEMS LIVED on Jericho Road in a red brick house that Nina Deem told me she wouldn't mind dying and coming back as.

"Nothing around here gets so much attention," she said, "except Meatloaf."

Maybe she told me this by way of apology for making me take off my boots before I followed her down the hall. Meatloaf, a fat red dachshund, licked my face and hands as I began praying my socks weren't going to smell.

I didn't get a really good look at her until I straightened up and let her lead me along polished wooden floors into the living room.

She was blond, like me, her hair falling to her shoulders, straight and shiny-soft. Green eyes to match the scoop-necked heavy green sweatshirt she wore. She had on jeans and some yellow Nike aqua socks, those shoe-sock things you can even wear into the water. Keats would wear them when we'd go clamming at the bay back on Long Island.

Meatloaf was waddling along behind us and Nina was saying, "Christmas? Dad didn't even let the tree in the house this year. It was out there on the sunporch"—waving her hand toward the long doors—"so we could see it, but the needles wouldn't drop to the floor. I mean, is that obsessive-compulsive or is that obsessive-compulsive? Really."

"We didn't have one," I said.

"One what?" She turned around and looked at me, waiting.

"A Christmas tree."

"Oh," she said, as though she'd forgotten she'd brought up the subject.

"We just had a lot of wreaths," I finished, feeling foolish for going on about it.

"We can sit here on the couch," she said, and Meatloaf took her up on the invitation, so I sat down beside him. We were a dachshund sandwich.

It was a large, comfortable room, lots of armchairs, and tables with flowers in vases, built-in bookcases all around, the same floors you could see your face in, but covered with old oriental rugs. Big, orange-and-brown pillows to go against all the beige-and-white slipcovers. In front of us a long, low table with a marble top, filled with the latest magazines. A single framed photograph of a blond woman in shorts, carrying a tennis racquet. Nina, fifteen years from then.

There was a notebook there, too, with a Flair pen stuck in its center.

"Do I call you John?" she asked.

"Everyone calls me Fell."

"As in fell down, fell apart, fell to pieces?"

"Or fell back on or fell on one's feet—it doesn't all have to be negative."

"Fell in love," she said. "Yeah, I guess there are good ways to fall, too . . . or you wouldn't be here."

"I don't follow you." I looked into her eyes for the first time. She wasn't shy about meeting someone's glance. Just the opposite. She was one of those we'll-see-who's-going-to-look-away-first types. So I looked away and added, "I don't get the part about I wouldn't be here if . . ." and I let my voice trail off. I was beginning badly, mainly because I didn't know what we were really talking about.

She let me know. She said, "If I hadn't fallen in love with Eddie, Dad wouldn't have called you to the rescue."

What was I supposed to say? Eddie? Who's Eddie? I don't know any Eddie?

I didn't say anything.

She said, "It's all right. I need tutoring, too, but Dad's an earhole sometimes. Really."

I had to laugh at the earhole bit. You couldn't say Nina Deem wasn't a lady.

"Everything you heard about Eddie Dragon is a lie!" she said.

"Fine. Let's get to work."

"We will, but remember that. He would never sell cocaine! He wouldn't even smoke pot with me when I asked him to!"

"Okay," I said. "I'm not arguing the point."

"Don't! He was the best thing that ever happened to me. He could no more sell dope than I could. He said it was a sure way to wreck your head."

"He was right about that."

She didn't press the point, I'll give her that. She leaned forward and got the notebook, opened it, and took out the Flair. "What I'm trying to do," she said, "what I want your help with, is this biographical essay I'm writing on Browning. I don't understand him."

"*Robert* Browning?"

"Is there a Walter Browning, a William Browning? Really. I thought you were supposed to be this dynamite writer."

"I'm not a dynamite writer," I said, while my greedy and materialistic mind raced ahead of me whispering: gold 7, word processor, six dollars an hour, don't mess it up, don't be an earhole. "I mean, I'm a good enough writer, and I certainly know Robert Browning. . . . I just thought I'd never have to read 'Fra Lippo Lippi' again, ever!"

She laughed. "You won't have to. I'm more interested in his life, and his romance with Elizabeth Barrett."

We were off and running. The air was clear, despite the odor that was now compelling Meatloaf to get all the way down on the floor and investigate my argyles.

When she finished reading aloud what she'd written, she said, "Rate it on a scale of one to ten."

"Eight."

"Why only eight?"

"It's very good, but you can't have sentences like 'Against all odds, these young lovers eloped in 1846.' "

"Why can't I?" Nina said, waving her arms in the air, and it was then that I saw it.

A tiny insect, a few inches above her left breast, coming out of her bra.

"You can't," I said, "because they weren't young. Elizabeth Barrett Browning was thirty-nine. He was thirty-four."

It wasn't alive.

"They couldn't have been that old, Fell!"

"They were," I said.

It was a tattoo of a pole-thin black what? With a long tail and deep-blue wings. A beetle.

"I don't believe you!" Nina said. Then she saw where my eyes were rooted.

"All right," she said, "we're not going to get anywhere until you take a good look!"

She grabbed the collar of her sweatshirt and yanked it down. "There! See it?"

"A dragonfly?"

"Good, Fell! A lot of slow wits think it's a mosquito or a beetle."

"Is it a permanent tattoo?"

"Yes. I found out where Eddie got his and I got one just like it. A fellow down in Lambertville does them. Like it?"

"It's an attention getter, all right."

"Only if you're with guys who look down your blouse," she said. "Let's get back to the Brownings."

She wasn't one to waste her father's money.

At five thirty, the grandfather clock in the hall gave a bong.

"Dad said to ask you to stay for dinner," Nina told me. "We eat at six, so we'll have another half hour if you can do it."

I said I could before I realized it was Wednesday, steak night at Sevens. She tossed back her hair and straightened her posture so the dragonfly disappeared. There was a phone in the hall by the clock, she said, if I wanted to call The Tower. "You won't miss out on the steak, either," she said, "because I had our butcher cut us a thick sirloin. . . . The only thing is, I haven't cooked a steak for ages! Dad's cut way back on red meat and I hardly ever eat it."

I jumped in. "I'll cook it!"

"Can you?"

I smiled. "How did you know we have steak on Wednesdays?"

"Dad. He was one of you, remember? . . . He wouldn't ask just anyone from The Hill to rescue me from Eddie. It'd have to be one of the holy Sevens, of course. Really."

"We're not that bad," I said.

"I know. You're a good tutor, Fell. Do me a favor?"

"I charge extra for favors."

"Let Dad think I don't know what you're really doing here—he hates it when I outsmart him."

"We're doing the Brownings so far as I'm concerned," I said. "Time out while I marinate the meat?"

10

MY FIRST DATE with Delia, I'd made her French toast. I was thinking about that while I reached up in the cupboard for seasonings to go in the marinade.

I was also thinking about the tattoo, and the look in Nina's eyes when she said Eddie's name.

I was beginning to be sorry for myself because I wasn't connected to anyone. It made me feel like a kid again, this half-assed (half-eared?) preppy who'd have to put his name on the blind-date list for The Charles Dance and hope the girl who got off the bus from Miss Tyler's school didn't have bad breath and think we ought to nuke Nicaragua.

Then I saw something that started me going the other way, and I began to grin while I grabbed it.

"Hey, Nina, where'd this come from?"

It was a bottle of Fox's U-Bet chocolate-flavored syrup. Made in Brooklyn!

"That was my mom's. It's about three years old. She used to order it by the case to make egg creams."

"Which I'd kill for! Do you happen to have any seltzer?"

"There's a cylinder in on the bar. Can you make an egg cream, Fell?"

"Can Michael Jackson dance?"

"I've tried to make them like she used to, but they don't come out right."

"Just leave everything to me. All I need now is that seltzer and some milk."

I finished marinating the steak while Nina got the cylinder, a carton of milk, and two glasses.

"Was that your mom's picture in on the coffee table?"

"Yes, but it's not good of her. She was beautiful. She was like some exotic hothouse flower daddy'd never let breathe fresh air. He's very overprotective, Fell."

"Sometimes you need protecting, Nina."

"*I* need it?"

"Not you in particular. We all need it sometimes."

"I get too much of it."

"I thought you said you'd like to come back as this house so you'd get some attention."

"That's right. This house gets loving care. I get locked inside with a bodyguard."

"How's this for loving care? Watch me," I said.

She stood there while I spooned an inch of Fox's U-Bet into each glass, adding another inch of milk.

"Is that all the milk you use? I use half a glass."

"That's too much. Now, the trick is to tilt the glass like so, and spray the seltzer off the spoon."

Soon there was a big chocolaty head.

"See?" I said.

We were right on the verge of clicking our glasses together in a toast I proposed to H. Fox & Company, Brooklyn, New York, when Meatloaf began crooning while he ran from the room as fast as his fat little legs could carry him.

"Dad's home," said Nina.

Dad was your average nice-man type, getting gray at the temples, but keeping himself lean, dressed in a brown suit, a guy who probably wore his necktie from the time he got up until he went to bed. He looked like he'd be at home in an office, a bank, a church, at Rotary, on the golf course, or on his way in first class to some Hilton hotel for a meeting.

If he'd started his business from scratch, as Schwartz had said, he was way past scratch now, and his voice let you know it.

"Nina, before we go in to dinner, I want you to change your top."

I automatically looked down at my own seedy sweater, scruffy jeans, and stockinged feet. Nina said, "Don't worry, Fell. Dad just doesn't like scoop necks."

"I don't have to look at it while I'm eating," Mr. Deem said.

"You don't ever have to look at it," said Nina. She finished the rest of her egg cream and left me in the kitchen with David Deem.

I told him I'd cook the steak, and he mouthed a few sentences about his cholesterol level finally getting down, and his triglyceride staying at about 150.

"You don't have to worry about all that yet, John."

I asked him to call me Fell, and if I should get the steak in right away.

He said Nina usually had the salad washed and waiting in the refrigerator, peeked in there, and nodded. "Yes, go ahead. Mrs. Whipple left us lima beans from last night we'll just heat up."

He got busy behind me, after he dropped the beans into a pan he put on low, but he didn't take his coat off or loosen his tie.

Meatloaf sat up and begged, and Mr. Deem tossed him something and told him to go into his bed.

Then Mr. Deem said, "I'm glad we have a few minutes alone, Fell. . . . If you ever hear anything or see anything that tells you Eddie Dragon is in touch with my daughter, I want you to tell me immediately. You know that, I hope."

Already I knew how hard this situation might become. I liked Nina. I couldn't see myself ratting on her. But I couldn't see myself letting her hang out with a pusher, either.

He went right on without waiting for any comment from me. "He's very clever, don't forget that. He can charm the birds down from the trees, too, so you have to be on your guard. . . . Did you see it?" he asked me.

"See what, sir?"

"The tattoo. You couldn't have missed it."

"I saw it." I liked it. I'd never tell him that, but I wouldn't have minded if Delia'd had something like it to remember me.

"He did that to her," said Deem.

"She said she did it on her own initiative."

He laughed unhappily. "Don't believe it! . . . Now she thinks it's zany and original. But imagine, Fell, years from now when Nina will want to attend a dance, or a dress-up dinner party, or go to the club for a swim: There it will be. He's marked her for life."

"Well, I'm sorry about that," I said.

"Then she talked about him, hmmm, Fell?"

"Not much. Just a little when I noticed the tattoo."

"What did she say?"

I sighed. I wasn't going to be good at this at all. "She just said anything I might hear about him is a lie."

"Ha! *He's* the liar! He's a pro, Fell! He had me believing him, and I've met my share of liars!"

The thought of it made him work the wooden fork

and spoon so vigorously, a piece of lettuce flew at my sweater.

I picked it off and popped it into my mouth. "Good dressing," I said. It needed salt and a touch more garlic, but it was surprisingly tasty. A great mustardy tang.

"My wife's recipe. . . . Did I see you two drinking egg creams?"

"Yes, sir."

"That's good. Nina says she can't make one right. They remind her of her mother too much, I think."

"She told me something about that."

"She did? She talked with you about her mother?"

"Not a lot, but a little."

"I'm surprised . . . and delighted. Nina has a lot of trouble talking about her. She took her death very hard. We both did, of course. Nina's so much like Barbara in every way, sometimes I walk into a room, see her, and have to stop and catch my breath. She's Barbara to her bones: the daredevil, the romantic—all the qualities I lack. But Nina could use some of my dull, old common sense, too. She needs to come down to earth."

I was timing the steak. "Mr. Deem? Do you two like your steak rare?"

"Yes, rare. . . . I'm glad you came on the scene, Fell. I know Nina will win you over, and you may feel disloyal if you have to report anything to me, but just remember this."

He stopped and came around so he could face me.

"If you care anything at all about my daughter, you'll

be doing her a very great service keeping Dragon out of her life."

Then his eyes got very wide and he said, "Oh, no!"

"What's wrong, sir?" I thought of cholesterol and triglyceride, of high blood pressure and heart attacks.

He went over to the sink and ran the cold water.

"Are you all right, Mr. Deem?" My own father had died very suddenly of a heart attack.

He grabbed a towel and put a corner of it under the water, turned, and handed it to me. "Your sweater," he said. "There's oil or something on it."

Where the lettuce had hit me.

I grinned with relief and dabbed at the stain.

"We should both have on aprons," he said.

Nina was definitely out to get him at dinner. She was pretending to be reviewing for him what we'd gone over during the tutoring, but she talked far more about Elizabeth Barrett than she did about Browning, harping on her controlling father.

"Ummm hmmmm," Mr. Deem would respond. "Well, Nina, they were very strict with young ladies in those days."

Nina gave me a triumphant look. Then she said, "Dad, when she met Robert Browning she was practically forty! Her father was *still* telling her what to do!"

"She was ill, wasn't she? Didn't you just say she was ill?"

"He made her think she was! He wanted to keep her home with him!"

"It all turned out all right, didn't it?"

"Yes, because she defied him! She eloped!"

"That's a word we don't use much anymore. Elope."

"Oh, we still use it, Dad. Those who have a reason to use it still use it."

She could have been talking about basket weaving in Madagascar for all the reaction she got out of him. He gave the same bland responses no matter how impassioned Nina became. He sneaked bits of steak to Meatloaf, who was stationed at his feet, under the table.

"The steak is done just right, Fell!" Mr. Deem decided to change the subject.

"Thanks, sir."

"Nina, did you show Fell any of your old stories?"

"I'm throwing them all out," she said. "They were from another time."

"You'll regret it if you do. You might want to remember that time someday, how you felt when you were younger."

"I don't want to remember feeling like this little Goody Two Shoes who raised her umbrella and heard the wind *sough* in the trees. I actually wrote that line, Fell. 'She raised her umbrella and heard the wind sough in the trees.' "

"Sough is a perfectly legitimate word," said her father.

"My future characters aren't going to own umbrellas," Nina said, "or slipcovers or coasters. I'm never going to write about careful people again!"

One thing I'd learned about her: If she *was* a jet crash,

she had a certain brave facade about her. I couldn't imagine her letting anyone feel sorry for her. I liked that about her, maybe because I was a little that way myself. We jet crashes had our pride.

I had to be back at The Hill by ten. At eight Mr. Deem walked out on the front porch with me, and we stood a moment in the cold night.

Then he grabbed my hand, and I felt his thumb push against my fingers. I had almost forgotten the Sevens handshake. I let my thumb touch his. It was an awkward gesture that made me feel silly, but he seemed satisfied.

"This is going to work out fine," he told me. "I can tell."

He went back inside and left the light on for me as I headed down the walk.

His Lincoln was there in the driveway.

The license plate read DDD–7.

The wind was soughing in the trees.

I COULD HAVE WALKED back to The Hill or caught the bus at the corner of Main and Hickory.

I thought of Dib and decided in favor of the bus. I

wanted to tell him all that Rinaldo had told me.

But a block before Hickory I turned into Playwicky Road.

While I'd been at the Deems', I'd forgotten Lasher and Creery. For all the luxury at Sevens, I'd missed cooking, and eating a meal in a quiet room where there was a female. I'd missed a living room and a four-legged creature padding around.

I remembered Jazzy dressed up as a question mark in a kindergarten play last Christmas. She'd had to recite some lines from Kipling:

I keep six honest serving men
(They taught me all I knew);
Their names are What and Why and When
And How and Where and Who.

Temporarily, anyway, I'd parked the six serving men at the curb, and reveled in the idea of being in a real home again.

⧈

Playwicky Arms was a row of two-story houses, each with its own twin entrances onto the street. The houses on the winding street were alternately gray and white, with brass lanterns in front and cobblestone sidewalks meeting the city's paved ones.

I wasn't looking for anything in particular, "just looking," as my mother was fond of saying in department stores.

Number 6 was white and in the middle.

Both the top and bottom floors were lighted. I figured Lauren must have gone from Sevens House to here, rather than catch the bus back to Miss Tyler's. Midwinter, during the week, there wasn't regular service to Princeton.

I was only slightly curious about this off-campus pad of Lasher's. It figured that he'd had one, and that only card players knew about it. He wasn't the first fellow from The Sevens to have one, probably just the first one to chance reprimand for poker or blackjack instead of girls.

What interested me more was the idea of surprising Lauren. I was trying to imagine that unflappable face reacting with surprise. It was a little like trying to picture the Mona Lisa throwing her head back to have a good belly laugh.

I enjoyed the idea of telling Dib I'd checked out Playwicky, too. He liked the image of Fell, Boy Detective, far more than he appreciated Fell, member of The Sevens. It would go a long way in helping him to stop suspecting I was part of some Sevens cover-up.

I walked up and down the street while I invented these excuses for my own chronic curiosity, and while I practiced what I'd say to Lauren.

Lauren, I can't stay but I finished assembling the memorial book, so can you pick it up tomorrow? I had my own selfish reasons, too. Sevens drew the line at free postage and delivery of packages. We had to get them to the post office ourselves, a chore I could easily postpone for weeks.

There were two bells at number 6, the top one with the name Lewis under it, the bottom one unmarked.

I pushed the bottom one, heard it ring, and waited.

My father used to say he could always feel it when he was being watched. It was a sixth sense. It had saved his life once when all he could see on a street where he was doing surveillance was an empty florist's station wagon with a roof rack carrying a coffin-sized cardboard box, the sort used for wholesale flower deliveries. There was a man with a gun inside the box, aiming at him through a hole. Dad ducked just in time, getting away in a crouch.

I could feel eyes on me from inside. I could see the curtains move in the downstairs front window. I knew there was no gun aimed at me, but some of the same feelings people who point guns have were probably overwhelming Lauren then. She'd say how did you find out about this place, Fell? I'd tell her I was in the neighborhood and number 6 just looked like her. Something about it.

I smiled at the thought and jabbed the bell again.

This time all the lights on the bottom floor went off. So did the one inside the brass lantern.

Plain enough. I walked away.

I went up the street in the opposite direction from where I'd entered it, and stood a moment beside a large oak tree, seeing if the lights would go on again.

I wondered if Lauren had seen that it was me, or if

she feared that it was someone who could cause trouble. Maybe over at Miss Tyler's the idea of her crashing in her brother's off-campus card den wouldn't sit so well. It probably wasn't the first time either. A girl like Lauren couldn't have been interested in cards. Boys, more likely . . . Rinaldo'd said to ask Kidder about number 6 Playwicky. What if Kidder, with his Colgate smile, his Polo wardrobe, and his Key West yacht, appealed to Lauren?

My thoughts were chasing in circles while I stood hugging myself to keep warm. I was ready to admit that my imagination was overtaking reality again. Kidder'd played poker there; whatever Lauren had been up to, I'd probably never know.

Staying was pointless, I decided. That was the second the lantern light went on again.

Just for a moment, a man stepped out and looked around.

I'd seen him before.

I'd never seen him barefoot, in an orange kimono, but I'd seen the thick white hair and the white mustache.

Only someone from Miami wouldn't think to pack slippers.

12

IN SEVENS HOUSE my mailbox was full. There was a large package from Mom, a letter from Keats, three messages from Dib. *Where are YOU?* was one. Then, *Where ARE you?* Finally, *WHERE are you?*

Mom never sent me stuff unless it was a special occasion. She said that since I'd made Sevens, sending me anything was like carrying coals to Newcastle.

I opened the package on the spot. Little plastic peanuts spilled from the box to the mailroom floor.

There were some bottles of Soho lemon spritzer, a jar of Sarabeth Rosy Cheek Preserves, and a box of David's Cookies. Things I loved and couldn't buy in Cottersville.

There were two white envelopes inside too.

I opened one and gulped. It was a valentine. It was the thirteenth of February. I'd forgotten Valentine's Day.

I knew the second envelope contained Jazzy's valentine.

I checked my Timex. Nine thirty. If I hurried, I could get over to Deem Library and make some home-made cards before mail pick-up at ten o'clock. At least they'd be postmarked the fourteenth.

Dib could wait a day for my news.

I shoved the package back into my box and headed for The Tower. Under the campus lights along the path, I read what Keats had written across a red heart.

Thanks for your postcard. Why would you read "Fra Lippo Lippi" when you could read Browning's "Confessions"?
How about this line, Fell?
"How sad and bad and mad it was—
But then, how it was sweet."
Does that remind you of us? Does anything?

XXXXX.

She was a freshman at Sweet Briar, down in Virginia, where February nights were never as cold and windy as the one I was hurrying through.

I'd call her with Valentine wishes. I couldn't do that with Mom and Jazzy. They liked getting theirs in the mail. Even late was better than none at all.

For a while I had the library to myself. I grabbed some cream-colored Sevens stationery and sat down at a table.

I folded one sheet and drew a heart across the front.

BE MY VALENTINE.

Inside I didn't get any more original.

Two hearts across the second one. Jazzy's name in one; mine in the other.

Only girlfriends inspired me, not my family. For Delia I'd have drawn the Taj Mahal, and written a verse in perfect iambic pentameter promising it to her.

The clock was striking ten when Rinaldo appeared. He wasn't in his usual uniform. I could see why Lasher's clothes hadn't thrilled him. He had on very tight black pegged pants, a black leather vest, a black-and-white silk shirt, and a black leather belt with a silver buckle. Black suede ankle boots . . . Lasher's style had alternated between classic preppy and baggy tramp.

"Closing time, Fell." Rinaldo put down the mail sack he was carrying, unlocked the CORRESPONDENCE box, and reached in for the letters there.

"Can you wait one second? I forgot Valentine's Day."

"Wait how long?"

"One second."

"One second's up." He walked toward me while I scratched the address across an envelope.

"You smell like a magazine, Rinaldo."

"I've got on Giorgio V.I.P. Special Reserve," he said. "You know what the ads say: Maybe one man in a thousand will wear it." He grinned. "That's me."

"Is it part of your inheritance?"

"No. Lasher—what did he wear? Something like Royal Copenhagen. This is sweeter! This gets the girls like honey draws bees. . . . I've got a date, Fell—crank it up."

"I'm done," I said. I handed the envelope to him. "Will it be postmarked the fourteenth?"

He nodded. "I'm dropping it off down there now."

I got up and walked along with him. The Tower clock was hammering out ten. In half an hour the dorm doors would be locked. It wasn't worth trying to get to Dib.

"I was on Playwicky Road tonight," I said, "and I saw something odd."

"Sniffing around?"

"I thought Lauren might be there. Instead, I saw

Creery's stepbrother come out of number 6."

Rinaldo snapped off the lights in the library. "I heard he's staying awhile."

"In Lasher's apartment?"

"That I didn't hear."

"You don't think it's odd?"

"Others used that place, Fell. It was for card playing, so why would Lasher's sister be there? . . . You are naive sometimes, you know." He picked up a black leather coat with a yellow quilted lining that was lying on the table outside the door. "Kidder went there. Other Sevens. You think it was a secret? Even you'd heard of the place."

Not until Rinaldo'd told me himself, but I skipped by that saying, "So Sevens arranged it?"

"A Sevens did, probably. Why not? This stepbrother of Creery's needs a place for a few weeks. Why wouldn't it be offered to him? That's what your Sevens is all about, isn't it? Something for nothing."

He snapped the hall lights off as we walked toward the front of The Tower. "Everything isn't suspicious, Fell, the way you think. You've got something on the brain, Fell." He flicked his fingers toward my head and laughed. Then he patted his heart with the same hand. "You need something here to occupy you. You should see what I'm going to occupy in about half an hour."

We went through the front door. Rinaldo had the mail sack over his shoulder. "Now if that little Porsche of Lasher's had been delivered early, maybe Rinaldo'd be heading off for the evening in style."

I gave him a smile. "I wouldn't worry."

"Yes, you would, Fell. Because you worry about everything, I'm learning. What you need is to have a girl."

"This is true," I said.

He feigned a punch at my chin. "You want me to fix you up with a townie?"

"Later," I said.

We waved and took off in opposite directions.

Then I called to him. "Wait, Rinaldo!"

He stopped.

I walked toward him. "Why is Creery's stepbrother staying for a few weeks?"

"You don't quit, Fell, do you?" He switched the mail-bag to the other shoulder. "He's staying until all this calms down."

"Until all *what* calms down?" I asked him.

"Maybe until *you* calm down, *compadre*. . . . I don't know why he's staying. I just know Creery's off the Sevens dinner list until the stepbrother leaves. Two weeks or so, he said."

Rinaldo turned to go. "*Hasta la vista*, Fell!"

I could almost hear Lasher's voice. *Hasta la vista, Flaco!*

"*Buena suerte*, Rinaldo!"

And the scream from just above us, I could hear. Still.

That night, as I was undressing, I found Jazzy's unopened valentine in my shirt pocket.

There was a picture of a white dog holding a red heart in its paws.

Inside it said, DOGGONE I LOVE YOU!

Jazzy'd printed something at the bottom in her usual style: large, crooked letters.

Johnny? Why is 6 afraid of 7?

There was an arrow pointing to the back of the card.

Turning it over, I thought of number 6 Playwicky Arms, and of Mark Twain's bare feet on the cold stone.

Because, Jazzy had continued, *7 8 9.*

13

ONE OF THE PERKS that went with keeping my eye on Nina Deem was getting to drive the second car. That's what both Nina and her father called the BMW, as if it had never belonged to anyone in particular, though I knew it'd been her mother's.

Deem had checked out my New York driver's license—he was a careful man. He'd advised me to get a Pennsylvania one, and to ask Dr. Skinner's permission. All done by the third week in February, when Nina talked me into taking her to New Hope for a poetry reading.

The roads were clear, and the sun was out, and even

though "Fra Lippo Lippi" had spoiled poetry for me forever, I liked to be behind the wheel.

I needed to get away from The Hill, too.

Late February, at Gardner, you crammed for tests, wrote papers on every subject from the design of the Parthenon to Romanticism's eighteenth-century beginnings, and took your S.A.T.'s over if you were trying to raise your score. I was trying to get mine out of the 500's.

I was also spending too much time working on The Charles Dance for The Sevens.

In between, Dib and I met when we could. And when we did, we fought.

He'd become convinced there was no way we'd ever figure out the true story of Lasher's death, that The Sevens had too much power. . . . He'd also teamed up with a scruffy group of townies, led by John Horner, a day student known as Little Jack. They drove around Cottersville in an old Mustang, no muffler, black, furry dice hanging from the mirror, six-packs iced in the backseat. . . .

"You've got your gang, I've got mine," he told me.

Neither of us had done anything about learning how to work the Smith-Corona PWP.

Creery's stepbrother was still with us, and Dib bought Rinaldo's explanation that it had been arranged through Sevens for him to stay in Lasher's apartment. He bought it, or he settled for it. He wasn't interested any longer in pursuing it, he said; he wasn't going to wait around in the dorm until I found time to discuss it with him.

The only change in Creery I noticed was his absence most nights at dinner. He ate with Lowell Hunter—that was Mark Twain's last name, Hunter.

◙

"Fell?" Nina said. "Thanks for this. I need to be around creative people." She liked to wear gear. She had on an old camouflage jacket several sizes too large for her, a sailor's blue knit cap pulled down around her long blond hair, and old corduroys that had been pegged so the cuffs slid into her lace-up leather boots.

"What's New Hope like? I hear it's a tourist trap."

Nina said, "Some people'd say it's a little artsy-fartsy, but in winter it's just another small town." She giggled. "With a lot of artsy-fartsy antique shops and restaurants. It's pretty, though."

"It's a reward for the A+ you got on your Browning paper."

"Thanks to you. You really improved it, Fell."

"I like your new stories"—most of them were fantasies about future worlds—"but I'd like to read your old ones, too."

She shook her head. "You never will. I burned them. They aren't me now. I'm not the same since Mom's death."

"You might want to remember what you were like, though."

"I *am* working on a story about my mother and father. Their last fight. You know what it was over? A croquet game."

"One was winning and one wasn't?"

"They weren't even playing," said Nina. "My father had this unpainted sample from DOT, our mail-order division. He was supposed to approve it. It was in his study when my mother found it. She was like a kid sometimes. She loved games! She wanted to put it out on the lawn immediately. Dad said she couldn't do it. He actually wrestled it away from her. It was weird, Fell: these two grown people tugging at a croquet set. He was shouting at her for unpacking it, and she was laughing at first. My aunt Peggy was visiting, and Mom was teasing him: Don't be a party pooper, Dave! Wait until you see my sister swing a croquet mallet! . . . But Dad was dead serious. No way were they going to set up that game! . . . I figured out why he didn't want her to set it up."

"Why?"

"It'd ruin the lawn. You know how he is. He didn't want the lawn spoiled. . . . It was a terrible fight, too. They'd never fought physically before. They used to make these conversational digs at each other, but this time he actually slapped her. Then she kicked him. Hard. My aunt Peggy tried to break it up, and she almost got hit too. . . . It's awful when parents fight, isn't it? I hated it!"

"My parents usually fought about my father's hours. He'd come through the door after a night's work, and Mom would say, Who are you? What are you doing in this house?"

Nina said, "And right after the fight over the croquet

set, she broke her neck doing a swan dive. Hit the shallow end of our pool because she'd overreached. If it wasn't so sad, I'd say it was how she'd have wanted to go. Doing something beautiful and wild."

"I'm sorry, Nina."

"Me too. . . . My aunt never forgave him. She thinks my mother was in shock from his slapping her . . . and over what? The fact my mother wanted to play a game on the lawn."

"It must be rough on him, too. Still."

"I know. I think of that a lot, because he truly did love her. She was such a passionate woman. He was always trying to curb her, not maliciously. He's not mean. But he just wants to be in control. . . . She loved romantic stories. She was always talking about famous lovers, reading us love poems at the dinner table. I think she was rubbing it in."

"What would he do?"

"Oh, Dad tolerated it. I think that was her way of getting back at him. He'd forget birthdays, anniversaries, and when he did remember them, he'd come home with something like a new microwave oven. . . . Emotion embarrasses him. She'd read us Keats, Shelley, some Frenchwoman named Duras. . . . My shrink says Vell, dot is a form of hostile displacement ven you do dot." She looked across at me and laughed, but I didn't. I suddenly remembered the lady in the long black mink coat at Lasher's funeral.

"What's your shrink's name?"

"Inge Lasher. You knew her son, didn't you? He was a Sevens before he took a dive off The Tower. Or am I not supposed to mention that?"

"I didn't know you knew about it."

"Dad didn't tell me. It wasn't in the newspaper, either. They always hush up bad stuff that happens on The Hill."

"Then how did you find out?"

"She told me. She said it vas not a disgrace so she vould not hide it. According to her, he secreted less growth hormone. Only she pronounces it groat hormone. Gawd, Fell!"

"What?"

"If your own shrink's son does himself in, how are you supposed to be helped by her?"

"You've probably got enough groat hormone."

"She hated having to tell me. She told all her patients. Clients, she calls us. She told everyone. It must have killed her! She tries to keep her personal life so secret. They all do. You're not supposed to focus on them. But I'd see her daughter sometimes. Right after Mom died, her daughter was living in their town house. During my session I'd see her out the window coming up the walk with her schoolbooks."

"Lauren," I said.

"Is that her name? I didn't even know her son was on The Hill until he died. What's Lauren like?"

"Sort of sophisticated."

"More than me?"

"You're not the same type."

"How is she different. Is she prettier?"

"No. You can't compare you two."

"Why not?"

"Why do you care?" I said.

"She's my shrink's daughter, Fell. You've never been shrunk, have you?"

"No."

"Well, we basket cases care about things like that."

"You should concentrate on yourself."

"I bet you're sorry you said that. That's all I do." Nina laughed. "I know Lauren's got inky-black hair. I remember that."

"And she wears Obsession, like an old girlfriend of mine." Sometimes I'd say things like that thinking Nina'd ask me questions about myself, but she didn't. She'd go right past the remark.

She said, "I like White Shoulders better. Would you date her, Fell?"

"She's too opaque for me."

"Opaque. Oh, I like that word." I'd just tossed out whatever'd come into my head, but Nina looked like I'd told her the combination for a safe full of gold. "Then she's exactly like her mother! I think Dr. Inge is the most mysterious person I've ever known! . . . And she's sophisticated, too. European. On the elegant side. But Fell, she's married to this little potbellied shrimp with a bald head. *You* should see *him*! He's nothing!"

"I have seen them. They were both at the memorial service."

"Of course! Then you know! Was it a sad memorial service?"

"There're not a lot of happy ones. But it was short." I decided not to mention that her shrink had addressed the gathering. It would save me having to go into all that. "No one from Sevens spoke—that was a little strange. Rinaldo, one of our houseboys, read a poem he'd written."

"I know Rinaldo! Rinaldo Velez?"

"Yes."

"He was a senior when I was a sophomore. I didn't know he wrote. I thought he only worried about things like not carrying stuff in his back pocket so he wouldn't ruin his bun line."

"I never noticed his bun line."

"When he dances? He looks just like Patrick Swayze in that old movie *Dirty Dancing*! Someday I'll show you his write-up in my yearbook."

"I'd like to see it."

She hurried back to her own priorities. "Well? Can you imagine those two shrinks married to one another?"

"Love is mysterious, Nina."

"I don't think marriage has anything to do with love, Fell. I think people settle."

"My parents were in love."

She did her usual bypass on the subject of me. "I'll never settle!" she said. "I'll never do what my mother did! I'll never let the man I marry control me. In fact, Fell, I may never *get* married! That story I wrote about a future world where marriage is for inferiors with low

I.Q.'s? I believe that! You don't have to get married to have children! Who says so? The law? Who cares about the law? You make your own laws, I believe!"

"Fine!" I said. "Now can we please talk about something *I'm* interested in?"

She looked surprised. "Okay. . . . Like what?"

"Like Spinoza's determinism," I said. "Or Descartes' dualism."

She gave my arm a hard punch. "Oh, Fell! You're good for me!"

I hoped so. There were times when we'd be talking about the future, about writing and Kenyon College over someplace like the University of Missouri's journalism school, and suddenly Nina would be out to lunch. Her eyes wouldn't move and her face lost its expression. I'd have to snap my fingers and say, Hey, come back.

But she was behaving less and less that way, and I liked to agree with her father, who'd always get me aside when he could do it tactfully and tell me I was helping her; he could see she was improving, forgetting Eddie Dragon.

Once she even said that herself, actually implying that I was better for her than Eddie. "It's good to get to know someone, isn't it, Fell?" She'd spoken up one afternoon. "I never really got to know a male except Dad, not really. I was always too nervous and self-conscious. God! After Eddie and I were together, I'd go over and over what we said, how I looked, play by play, like my whole life depended on some dumb little interlude with him. But this is just us: easy, relaxed. It's good like this. It's better."

She'd even stopped saying "really" in every sentence.

We rode in silence for a while, following the Delaware River, which had chunks of ice floating in it, and Nina leaned over and snapped on the radio. She pushed the button to find music that suited her. She was sort of jumping around in the seat, taking her cap off to shake her hair free, putting it back on. She seemed to be acting out everything I was feeling: It was a great day, good to be away from Cottersville, pretty out there with the sun inching over to sink down in the sky, neat that the radio was playing old Elvis stuff.

When we got to the coffee shop where the Friday-afternoon poetry readings were held, there was a sign on the door:

CLOSED FEBRUARY AND MARCH.

"Didn't you *call*, Nina?"

"Would we be here if I had? Don't get mad at me. How do you think *I* feel?"

"Sorry," I said. "What'll we do now? Is anything open?"

We stood there hugging ourselves and stamping our feet in the cold, and Nina said unless I wanted to look at sleigh beds or weather vanes circa 1800, we were out of luck.

"I'm not hungry, either," she added.

"I guess we'll just drive back. No movies?"

"No movies." She was heading toward the car. "It's too cold to walk around."

"Didn't you know they closed in winter?"

"Fell, quit nagging me. Let's try to look at the doughnut and not at the hole."

I opened the car door for her and said I wouldn't mind looking at a doughnut, either—I hadn't eaten since lunch.

When I got back behind the wheel, she said to drive up near Point Pleasant. She thought there was a hamburger place that way.

She directed me while I tried to get myself back in a good mood. I knew the reason I was sounding cranky was that I was disappointed. I rated poetry readings about the same as guided tours through flower gardens, but at least it would have been special to Nina, something she'd remember us doing together. . . . It'd been a long time since I'd cared about pleasing a girl. I wasn't sure how much of it had to do with my wanting her to get her bearings again, or how much it had to do with me being ready to crank up my own broken motor. Something was in the wind . . . and it was a relief from thoughts of a body falling, a voice shrieking, and unanswered questions that had caused a rift between Dib and me.

We listened to the radio for a while: golden oldies—The Beatles and Steppenwolf, Jimi Hendrix and Buffalo Springfield.

Finally she glanced my way and said she had an idea.

"What?"

"You're still mad, aren't you, Fell?"

"I'm over that. I wasn't really mad. . . . What's your idea?"

"I want to see something."

"What?"

"Something up ahead here."

"Food, I hope."

"Not food. . . . He's got a shop somewhere right near here," she said. "His sister runs it. He won't be there, so don't worry."

She waited for it to sink in.

It hit my stomach first, then traveled around in my gut for a while and settled in my windpipe.

When my voice returned, it said, "You planned this all along, didn't you, Nina?"

"And don't say my name in there," she said. "I promised him I'd never come here." She touched my leg with her hand. "Oh, Fell, this won't hurt anything. I'm just curious. Aren't you ever curious?"

I was staring straight ahead, mad as hell, when I saw it come into view.

A gigantic black dragon with gold wings and green eyes, breathing out fake fire.

14

DRAGONLAND WAS AN OLD, gray, cold, musty-smelling barn at the bottom of a hill. It was one of those hodge-podge places that sold everything from Pennsylvania Dutch hex signs to leather coats with fringe on the sleeves. They specialized in twenty-four-hour film service, "Award-Winning Wedding and Graduation Photography," "Furniture: Bought and Sold," and rental tools.

The giant dragon perched on the roof wasn't the only one. Dragons were everywhere, in every color, made of rubber, iron, tin, wood, and papier mâché. There were dragonflies, too. If Eddie Dragon didn't run the place himself, his spirit certainly dominated the decor.

At one end of the barn there was a mural of a waterfall, an old mill, and a willow tree, an iron bench in front of it. A sign to the left saying:

DRESS UP IN OLD CLOTHES
TAKE HOME A SOUVENIR.

I'd seen the scenery before, in the photograph of Eddie Dragon that Schwartz had given me.

To the right there was a rack with assorted clothes, feather boas and hats with veils, canes, top hats, derbies, old furs and mustaches and wigs.

There was a woman behind the counter with the kind

of great, warm smile that could make you forget anything, including the fact you shouldn't have stopped the car to go inside that place with Nina.

She didn't look like someone who belonged in a Pennsylvania winter. I could see her out under the sun in some Kansas field with a piece of straw stuck playfully between her teeth and the wind blowing back her thick, curly, brown hair. She had magnificent white teeth; big everything: hands, feet, bosoms, the gypsy type loaded with beads and bracelets jangling on her wrists. She had on a long, red dress with a full skirt and some kind of Mexican-looking red-and-white shawl over her shoulders. You'd imagine her stirring pots of fabulous-tasting stews, or tending a garden, or mending something. She might as well have had one of those cartoon balloons over her head with "I'll take care of you" inside.

It was hard for me to guess women's ages. All the while I was with Delia, I thought she was maybe nineteen—she'd never tell me. She was really twenty-five. This woman looked older. I figured she was Dragon's big sister.

"You lost?" she said. "You look lost." She was laughing, picking up a Siamese cat who'd run to her with his ruff up the moment the bell jingled to announce our arrival.

I'd seen the cat before, too. I let Nina do the talking.

"We were really looking for someplace to get a hamburger."

"Not around here, I'm afraid. Try New Hope down the road. Or Doylestown up the road."

"You have a lot of interesting things."

"We try. . . . Are you visiting?"

"We came from New Jersey," Nina said. She wasn't one to worry that there was a Pennsylvania license plate on the BMW.

The cat was hanging on to the woman like we were going to bag it and toss it in the river. She got its claws out of her shawl and put it down on the floor. "Go find your mousie," she said to it, as though the thing would answer Okay! Good idea! and the dark-brown tail disappeared into a room behind her. No door, just a curtain of beads.

"Would you like me to show you anything?"

"I just *love* this place!" Nina sounded naive and girlish, instead of dark-hearted and possessed.

The woman gave us that great big white smile again and said, "I'm Ann."

Nina jumped right in. "I'm Lauren," she said, "and that's John Fell."

"Lauren, John," Ann said. "If you want to know the price of anything, there's a tag on the bottom."

"Fell, let's have our picture taken!" Nina said.

Ann said, "Just pick out your costumes. Anything over on the rack."

Nina headed that way, babbling about how we'd have a souvenir of the day, and soon she'd found herself a little green hat with an orange feather on it, a black velvet cape, and a white silk parasol.

"Ready!" she said.

I walked over, put on the top hat and a long black

coat with a fur collar, grabbed a black cane to complete the costume.

Ann was standing there with her hand on her hips laughing and *oh*ing and *ah*ing. As soon as we moved toward the iron bench in front of the mural with the mill, and the waterfall and the willow tree, she picked up a camera.

"I'm doing all the hard work now," she said, "while the boss is on assignment."

"Who's the dragon collector?" Nina asked.

"My husband. Eddie," Ann said. "That's our last name. Dragon."

I gave Nina a long, long look she refused to return, so I figured she was handling it Nina style: no show of the punch that must have just landed hard to her insides.

She was busy acting as though this was one of the best times she'd ever had, twirling her parasol, and affecting a haughty expression. "Let's try and look très, très superior," she said to me, something I would have expected from Lauren Lasher, never Nina.

I tried my best: tilting my top hat over my eye, resting my weight on the cane, my arm around Nina.

"That's jaunty, not superior," said Nina.

Ann just kept laughing.

Nina fixed the top hat so it sat squarely on my head, and she told me to stare straight ahead and hook the cane over my free arm.

"Good, Lauren!" Ann said. "That's fun!"

"Now don't smile and don't put your arm around me. I'll hook mine in yours," Nina directed me.

"Perfect!" Ann said. "It'll be ready in no time."

The cross-eyed Siamese was watching us behind the beads in the doorway.

Nina walked around looking at things I didn't want to look at, like rugs made out of animal skin and carvings made from elephant tusks.

I said, "You've really got a lot of variety."

"My husband's a pack rat. I never know what he'll walk in with, but it's always different." She laughed again. She was a hard laugher, tossing back her head, showing her love of life . . . and of Eddie Dragon, too, I thought.

I asked her what we owed her, and as soon as she'd given me five dollars change from a twenty, the picture was ready. It came in a small metal frame, with REMEMBER POINT PLEASANT written in gold at the top.

It wasn't good of me. I looked the way I'd begun to feel: like someone getting used to a bad smell.

Nina was a better actress. She came off looking haughty, superficial, insane.

"This has been fun!" Nina said, but the air was seeping out of the balloon: I could see it in her tired little smile, the kind that began to hurt the corners of your mouth because of all the effort that was going into it.

While Ann walked us to the door, she said, "Goodbye, Lauren, John. Thanks for stopping by. It gets lonely here this time of year."

15

WE WERE DRIVING along the river's edge. I put the fog lights on.

"He told me not to go there," she said softly.

"I can see why."

"Fell? I never, *ever* want to see him again!"

It was easy to ignore that one.

I snapped, "What's this crap about him being on assignment? She made him sound like a foreign correspondent or something."

"He takes pictures. Weddings and stuff."

"How come you knew he wouldn't be there today?"

She didn't answer for a minute. Then she said, "I called there yesterday. I pretended I wanted him to take some baby pictures, and she said he was on assignment until next Monday."

"You've been calling him all along, then?"

"No. I never dared call him there. I wouldn't have known about that place, except when he got framed the address was in the newspaper."

"When he got framed. Sure."

"He got framed, Fell."

"And his *sister* runs the place. Sure."

"How do you think *I* feel, Fell? Believe me, I am *finished* with Edward Gilbert Dragon!"

"*Believe* you," I laughed.

"Don't you have any feelings for me?"

"Yeah. I have the feeling you've just forced me to become an informer."

"You're not going to tell Dad?"

"I'm not? Why aren't I? Dad's paying me."

"I didn't try to *see* Eddie, Fell. I didn't even want to see him. I just wanted to see Dragonland. . . . He'd never take me there."

"I'm not surprised."

"Fell, *please* don't tell Dad! I can promise you I'll never have anything to do with Eddie Dragon again!" She turned to face me, pulling her knees up under her, slinging an arm across the seat. "Listen to me, Fell! I feel *horrible!* She's so . . . earnest."

"She's a lot more than earnest!"

"Do you think she's pretty?"

"Yes, I think she's pretty, and if the next question is do I think she's prettier than you, yes! And smarter, too!"

She touched my shoulder with her hand. "Oh, Fell, don't be mad. I'm trying to handle this thing, and I can't deal with it when you're mad at me."

"Tough!" I said. "Damn! Everything was going so well, I thought, and all the while you've got these snakes in your head!"

"That's a good name for them, snakes. Dr. Inge calls them compulsions, but they're snakes all right. They *were*, anyway."

She touched the bare skin at my neck with her finger. "Fell? Please? I'm sorry."

"And don't try stuff like that!" I said.

"I'm just touching you, friend to friend."

"Don't!" I said. I leaned over and pushed on the radio. "I don't want to talk, okay?"

⊡

When we got to Cottersville, the black Lincoln was in the drive. The porch light was on. The downstairs lights, and a light where David Deem had his study.

I locked the BMW and handed the key to Nina. She gave me the souvenir photograph. "I don't want this thing—do you?"

I stuffed it inside my jacket.

We were standing in the driveway. Meatloaf was barking. She pulled off her stocking cap and shook her hair loose so the moon caught its shine.

"It was really good that we went there, Fell. Now I know the truth. . . . Can't you at least think about not telling Dad? Sleep on it or something? I'm in little pieces right now."

"I'm not going to tell him tonight," I said. "I'm too hungry."

"You're always hungry." She was starting to cry.

"Nina," I began, not knowing where it would end, not having to worry because the front door opened and her father stepped out on the porch. "Come in, Fell! Mrs. Whipple made you both corned beef sandwiches."

"Please don't tell him, Fell," Nina said.

⊡

I said I couldn't stay, I'd take my sandwich with me, and David Deem picked up Meatloaf and told me what he had to say wouldn't take long.

"You go into the kitchen and wrap Fell's sandwich, honey," he told Nina. "Fell? Come in and sit down for a minute."

Then he said, "Do those boots come off?"

⊡

I was in my smelly stockinged feet again, my jacket over my lap, sitting forward on the couch.

"You've never told me how you like being a Sevens," said Mr. Deem, straightening his tie, leaning back in an armchair he was sharing with Meatloaf.

"Who wouldn't like it?" I said.

"Take me. I was this raw-eared kid from Pennsylvania Dutch country, father a farmer. I went to The Hill on a scholarship. I'd always made my own bed, didn't know what a soupspoon was, never, never had anyone wait on me . . . and suddenly . . ." He spread his arms out.

"That was all changed by mere chance," I said.

He laughed hard at that. "Yes . . . yes . . . it changed my life, Fell. It gave me my first taste of being somebody."

I let him talk. I didn't think it was the right time to tell him "somebody's" daughter was still sneaking around after a pusher who suddenly had a wife in the bargain.

"I feel badly about what happened at The Tower." He lowered his voice to a whisper. "The suicide. I haven't told Nina. It just so happens that was her psychiatrist's son."

"Nina knows, Mr. Deem. Dr. Lasher told her."

He thought that one over. He said. "Nina's so interior.

She calls *me* secretive because I lock my study. But look at her. You think she'd have told me she knew."

I resisted saying No, I wouldn't think that. I would think Nina wouldn't tell anything . . . and here's why, Mr. Deem.

"Her doctor overdoes the confidentiality rule, if you ask me. Here I've been so careful about keeping all that business to myself. Is Nina taking it all right?"

"Your daughter seems to handle things," I said.

"Yes. That's her mother's independent streak. . . . Well, then, this clears the way for what I'm about to suggest. I'd like Nina to meet some nice young men now that the dragon's been slain." A pleased little haw-haw for punctuation.

I bit my lip. I'd hear him out first. I was thinking of the corned beef sandwich, too. I was hoping Mrs. Whipple knew enough to smear the bread with lots of Dijon mustard.

"The best young men are on The Hill, no doubt of that. And from what I see of you, Fell, Sevens is still instilling in its members the idea that you live up to privilege, and become more because of it."

How was I going to tell him I'd become less the second I saw Dragonland? I'd become Silly Putty in Nina's hands.

"One of the most amusing and memorable traditions of The Sevens, of course, is The Charles Dance. What fun I had at those things!" He was stretching his legs out, letting Meatloaf wiggle onto his lap. "Do you know that at the first Charles Dance there were twelve boys dressed the same as me? Never go as Charlie Chaplin, Fell. You'll see yourself all over the place!"

"I was thinking of going as Damon Charles."

"Uh-oh, the founder himself, hmmm? That takes nerve. . . . I like that, Fell. I wonder if anyone's ever done that?"

"In his pictures he has a big handlebar mustache and a monocle . . . so it'll be easy."

Nina was back in the room, arms folded across her chest, an uncertain look in her eyes, directed at me.

"Mustard, Fell?" she said.

"Yes. Dijon?"

"Dijon. It's already on both sandwiches. I'd have had to make you another if you didn't like it. . . . Well?" She shrugged. "Is this a private conversation?" She couldn't seem to look at her father.

"Not really, Nina, honey," he answered her, and his tone of voice told her I hadn't squealed . . . yet.

Then he said, "I checked with The Sevens today and learned that Fell's signed up for a blind date for The Charles Dance."

He glanced across at me. "You don't have to take a *blind* date, Fell, if you'd prefer to take Nina. I'm ready for her to see how The Sevens do things."

"Oh, Dad! Can I go?"

"Well, Fell?" said Mr. Deem.

Both of them were looking at me expectantly.

"Sure," I said. What was I supposed to say? "Would you go with me, Nina?"

"I'd like that, Fell."

"It'll be her very first time on The Hill," said Mr. Deem. "I wanted it to be for something Sevens was doing. This is perfect."

"Perfect!" Nina agreed. "Oh, I hope and pray nothing comes up to spoil this!"

Her father chuckled. "Such histrionics, Nina! You *hope* and *pray?* . . . Nothing's going to spoil this. What could spoil it?"

Then he said, "I know you're hurrying, Fell, and Nina's occupied a lot of your time today, so take the BMW. It's cold, too."

"I can hike it," I told him.

"Anyone can hike it, but what's being a Sevens all about? . . . Take advantage of your advantages, Fell. You can bring the car back tomorrow afternoon." Then, meticulous as always, he added, "I told you before, didn't I, that there's a spare key in the back ashtray?"

Nina walked me to the door. "I feel like a spare female. You don't have to take me to the dance if you don't want to," she said. "I know Dad sprang that on you in a way you almost couldn't refuse."

"He sprang it on you, too," I said. I was getting into my boots and thinking about buying myself some Odor-Eaters for the insides, if I kept visiting the Deems.

"He didn't spring it on me, exactly. I've been begging him to ask you to invite me."

I was glad, too glad, the kind of glad that leaps up the way Wordsworth's heart did when when he beheld a rainbow in the sky.

"If today hadn't happened," I started to say, and she

didn't let me finish. She put two fingers against my lips.

"Today was the tag end of something. The Fates arranged for today to happen."

"*You* arranged for today to happen, Nina."

"It was like the final period at the end of the sentence 'I don't care about him anymore.' "

"Just say the period. Never mind the final period."

"My tutor." She smiled at me, coming closer.

I moved back a step, remembering the dragonfly with the blue wings crawling out of her bra.

I said, "Why do I still have the feeling I can't trust you?"

"I'll make that go away. You'll see."

She was looking all over my face, and I could feel something shivering down my arms.

Her hands reached up, starting to rest on my shoulders, but I shrugged them away, trying to act the way someone would when he was still angry.

It wasn't easy.

Maybe my problem was I liked tricky females. I didn't have a history of elevated heartbeat except when I was confronted by the beautiful/sweet-talking/kinky ones who made chopped liver out of your heart.

She handed me the keys to the BMW, and I went outside where winter was waiting to cool me off.

16

ALL I WANTED to do that night was eat my sandwich in peace and study for the test on medieval history coming up Monday. I'd be expected to explain, in an hour, how a scruffy army of illiterate soldiers, chomping on hunks of raw meat between battles, could bring down the whole Roman Empire.

Sevens House was dead. It seemed as though everyone but Mrs. Violet, our housemother, was still over at The Tower. I looked at my watch. It was almost eight. They were finished with dessert by now, those who hadn't left for the weekend. Some were still hanging around over coffee, or starting to play chess and backgammon in the library. Others were on their way into Cottersville, to meet the bus from Miss Tyler's or to go to the movies, bowling, the play at the Civic Center.

I got my mail. That was when I noticed someone else abroad in Sevens House. Creery. Behind me in the phone booth. He wasn't dining at The Tower these nights. He looked like he'd just come in from the cold, too.

I could hear him telling someone, "I waited over an hour for you. Ask Lowell. Where were you?"

I opened a club bill for the gold 7 I'd already sent to Mom. OVERDUE was stamped across it.

"Then I'll come there tomorrow morning," Creery

continued. . . . "Not too early because I'll be up late."

I didn't have any personal letters. I never opened my box that I didn't hope I'd see one from Delia. I was going to hear from Delia the day they discovered something that would rhyme with orange, but that never stopped me looking for the tiny handwriting with the long loops and the T bars flying off the handles.

I had the usual junk mail: Save the Seals and Support National Arbor Day. Your Christmas subscription to *Esquire* will be up next December so renew in March. A catalog from The Sharper Image promising that a Shotline Putter would release the pro golfer within me.

I tossed it all in the wastebasket while Creery told whoever he was talking to that he had to cram for the same history test. I decided to keep him in mind if we were called on to describe Alaric the Goth, the one who plundered Rome and got everyone eating each other instead of the parrots' tongues they were fond of baking into pies.

I did wonder who Creery'd have in his life to complain to, since it wasn't his stepbrother on the phone. And I thought about who he might be meeting "there" next day . . . maybe the same one who arranged for Lowell Hunter to stay at number 6 Playwicky.

"How are you, Fell?" said Mrs. Violet. "Long time no see."

Our housemother was always in white, always gorgeous, usually stationed nights in the wing chair near the reception room.

"I'm fine, thanks. What are you reading tonight?"

She closed the book in her lap so I could see the cover. *Hunted Down* by Charles Dickens.

"You want to hear something extraordinary?" she said, not waiting for my answer. "Listen. *I have known a vast quantity of nonsense talked about bad men not looking you in the face. Don't trust that conventional idea. Dishonesty will stare honestly out of countenance, any day in the week.* She pushed a strand of blond hair away from her forehead and looked up at me. "And I always judge boys by whether or not they can look you in the eye."

"Maybe Dickens didn't mean boys," I said. "My dad used to say a really good con man always looks you in the eye."

So had Delia had that skill. So did Nina.

"I'll have to think about that," Mrs. Violet said.

Creery was going up the staircase in a long gabardine overcoat, the blue-and-white wool Sevens scarf wrapped around his neck, the tail behind his head.

It wasn't like him to greet Mrs. Violet. It wasn't like his eyes to see the people around him. His eyes saw La La Land, little blue and red pills, joints and smoke.

"Fell? That friend of yours from the dorm was in your room earlier this evening. He said he had permission."

"He does, ma'am."

"Sidney Dibble."

"Yes."

"And your mother called. She said it wasn't important. Just a hello."

Mom had probably received the gold 7 for her birthday.

I thanked Mrs. Violet and kept going. In a while her freshman groupies would come over from The Tower. A score of them. Healthy young boys who turned into groveling lackeys, eager to do any chore she could dream up. Or they simply sat at her feet while she read to them. It didn't matter what. She'd call them "darling" or "dear"—words most of them never heard from any lips but hers, unless they called home.

When I got up to my room, I saw that Dib had left a red 7 hanging on my doorknob. All Sevens were issued one, which we could hang there when we didn't want to be disturbed. No one in Sevens House went through a door with one on it.

I pocketed it as I went inside.

The living room was dark, but I could see through to the bedroom, where there were green letters lit up on the face of the word processor.

I switched on a light and got out of my coat. I grabbed a Soho lemon spritzer from the refrigerator.

I supposed Dib had left me a message For My Eyes Only, probably something against Sevens, me . . . me and Sevens.

I wanted to relish the corned beef sandwich before I read it. I wanted to think a minute about Nina. Gather ye rosebuds while ye may, someone wrote. Not the same one who wrote Duty before pleasure.

There was just enough Dijon on the bread. I was too

hungry to care that the bread was white and fell into the empty-carbohydrate category, too ravenous to regret it wasn't rye or pumpernickel. Too starved to miss a fat dill-and-garlic pickle.

I began demolishing it, still standing, which is the only honest position for rationalizing. All I'd agreed to do was report back to David Deem if Nina tried to see Dragon. Technically, she hadn't tried to *see* him, only Dragonland . . . Chances were that what she'd found there *would* be enough to discourage her from ever wanting to see him again.

I played it back a few times and it didn't have a discordant note.

My dad would have said it was too pat.

But my dad hadn't arrived at his judgments when he was seventeen, horny, and far from Brooklyn.

I finished the sandwich and carried my bottle of lemon spritzer in toward the green letters.

Dear Lionel,

The enclosed copy of a letter from Cyril Creery to his stepbrother is self-explanatory.

I think you will agree that this is more serious than anything that has ever been handled in Twilight Truth, although ideally it should be done in that manner. However, it is unlikely, as you'll see in the fifth paragraph, that Creery would ever on his own allow it to be used in that ceremony.

The letter came into my hands because a concerned outside party knew the information in it was vital to

Sevens. I make no apologies for passing it on to you, since the honor of Sevens has, for me, always had priority over any other principle.

I've held on to this since Christmas, weighing what course to take. Surely this calls for The Sevens Revenge . . . and for the immediate ouster of Cyril Creery from our organization.

Sincerely,
Paul Lasher

Lasher's letter had been written three days before his death.

I reached up and switched on my desk light.

Dib had left a note on my blotter.

It wasn't a tutorial inside—it was a regular microwafer I came upon when I pushed Microwafer Directory and found LETTERS.

There are others there: complaints to stores, and one to his father about the delivery of the Porsche, but nothing pertinent.

They are all permanently stored, so just pull the microwafer out, turn the two switches off, and CALL ME.

Dib

I called him.

"What do you think Creery's letter could have said, Fell?"

"How would I know?"

"And what about The Sevens Revenge? You said it was a myth."

"I thought it was. It's news to me, too."

"Sure. Surprise, surprise."

I couldn't convince him that I was as much in the dark as he was, but we made a date to meet in the morning.

I fell asleep reading about the Crusades and dreamed that Nina was handing me Creery's letter. Then her face turned into Delia's, and she said, "Surprise, surprise, Fell."

17

SATURDAY MORNING.

Nobody'd ever warned me about winters in Pennsylvania. The cold sky hung heavy above me, like some enormous net over a ballroom loaded with balloons waiting to be freed with the jerk of a rope, only snow would pour down. Everyone walking along the streets had little white clouds puffing out of them, their postures bent and huddled into benumbed bones. I had the heater going full blast; ditto the radio: warming up with INXS, Big Pig, and John Cougar Mellencamp.

I cruised up and down Playwicky Road. It was narrow and twisting, with few trees save for the oak I'd stood behind the night I'd seen Lowell Hunter come out of number 6.

Anyone on foot would be seen immediately in the daytime.

Most of the apartment houses had parking lots behind them. There were few cars. Those that parked out front were also too conspicious for any serious surveillance.

I headed for the nearest supermarket, where you were most likely to find boxes of all shapes and sizes.

Dib was standing in front of the dorm when I pulled up at eight. He hadn't expected me to arrive in a car. I had to beep the horn. He ran toward me layered in a turtleneck, a shirt, a crew-neck sweater, a parka. Levi's, boots, his old navy-striped Moriarty hat pulled down over his ears.

"Where'd you get the wheels?"

While I told him, and he interrupted to say he *had* to have something cold to drink, I got the first blast of a breath that could probably have killed little flying things as easily as anything Black Flag made.

"There's a store down on Main near the bus stop. You can get a Coke there."

"And aspirin," said Dib.

"How did you tie one on in the dorm?"

"I went out for an hour after your call."

"With your gang?"

"Just Little Jack. You don't mind if I have a little fun too, do you? . . . Where are we headed?"

"The only thing I can think to do is follow the one lead we have, while I have a car."

"Lasher's letter is the one lead we have."

"I'm talking about Playwicky Road now."

"Let's talk about why Lionel Schwartz didn't mention that letter to the police."

"Dib, we went over that last night. He might have mentioned it, and they might have their reason for keeping it quiet."

"I think Sevens is keeping it quiet."

"You told me what you think. Now let me take a look at number six Playwicky and see who's meeting Creery there."

"I'm not in any shape to sit around watching an apartment when we don't know what we're looking for."

"You don't have to watch it. You have to help set me up. Then you can go back to the dorm and sack out."

"I might even have to puke," he said.

He wasn't kidding. He looked pale. He was rubbing his stomach the way you'd soothe some frightened animal.

"What's the big box in back?" he asked.

"I'll explain that later. . . . Dib, you look and stink like something died in you."

"Cork it, Fell! I'm just hung over."

"What's going on with you? Do you drink a lot, or was last night a first?"

"We go out."

"Where do you go when you go out?"

"Around, Fell. What difference does it make to you? I have to have other friends."

"You can get yourself expelled—that's the difference it makes to me."

"Unlike you, hmmm?"

"Maybe I can't get expelled, but I can't get away with drinking either. We're self-regulatory, but the bottom line's the same."

" 'Just a song at twilight,' " Dib sang off-key.

"Well, it's better than getting the boot. You're asking for it, Dib."

"You've swallowed Sevens hook, line, and sinker, Fell."

"I don't even hang out with them! I'm so busy tutoring a townie, it took *you* to bring that letter out of the machine."

"What about the gold 7 you got your mom?"

"I got it for *her,* not for me."

"My mom wouldn't wear one of those things, even if I was in Sevens. She doesn't buy designer clothes, either, and not because she can't afford to. She says she's not a walking advertisement for Calvin Klein or Gucci."

"Yours has been around more than mine. Mine's easily impressed, maybe."

"*You're* easily impressed, Fell."

"I'm not easily asphyxiated, or your breath would have killed me two blocks back."

We both began to laugh.

The tension that had started crowding us was broken. At Main Pharmacy he bought some Binaca for his breath and a couple of cans of cold Sprite.

A block before Playwicky Road, I pulled over to the curb.

"I learned this from my father," I said. "He'd do this when he was staking out some place they were dealing drugs. We're going to put that big box back there up where you're sitting, and I'm going to get inside it. See where I cut the holes?"

He gave a look. "What am I going to do?"

"After I get inside the box, you're going to drive up in front of the house. You're going to leave me under the box. You can catch a bus back near the pharmacy."

"So it'll just look like a car with a box in it."

"Right. . . . When my father'd be watching a crack house, sometimes he'd be stuck inside for a whole afternoon. He'd take along a wide-neck water bottle to piss into."

"Neat, Fell! And you'll be all right by yourself?"

"Why not? I'm just going to watch the place. Maybe I won't see anything important. But I want to try and find out who's there besides Creery and Lowell Hunter."

"It'll be a Sevens, for sure, and what'll that tell you?"

"I'll know when I know."

"And you're going to tell me when you know?"

"Yes. I'm going to tell you."

"Is that a promise?"

"It's a promise."

"Because it'd be easy for you to lie."

"I'm not going to. We're in this together."

Dib chugalugged a Sprite.

He said, "What happens when you've seen what you came down here to see?"

"I slip out from under and drive off. I don't care so much about being seen *after* I find out who the third party is, I don't think. . . . But this way I can choose my time to exit the scene."

We got out of the BMW and began putting the plan into action.

Before I got up under the box, I said, "Anything you've got to say to me, say now. When you pull up and park, you get out fast and walk away."

"I'll meet you back at the dorm. What time?"

"Hard to say. I have to return the car."

"I'm going to sack out anyway, so I'll be in my room all afternoon."

"I'll call you when I'm back on The Hill."

It was twenty minutes to nine.

"You're going to freeze your ass," said Dib.

MY FATHER USED TO CALL that kind of surveillance B.S. He meant Box Surveillance, but he meant B.S., too, because that's what it was, a real crappy detail. You couldn't eat, glance at a newspaper, listen to tapes, or do anything but ache to scratch all the parts of you suddenly itching in violent protest at what you were doing. Your body also gave you two-minute spots of coming attractions if you kept it up: arthritis, headache, muscular aches and pains, constipation, urinary incontinence: the gamut.

Sometimes he'd come home from B.S. filled with ideas of how our lives were going to change. Mom wasn't going to work for a caterer anymore, she was going to become one. Since I loved cooking so much, I was going to apprentice myself to some famous chef in a fancy New York restaurant. Jazzy would go to day care. Dad would turn down any future assignments that might involve crack houses. We were going to shape up as a family. . . . Sure, because that's what you do under a box. You promise yourself you'll never be under another one. You begin making grandiose plans for yourself, and for everyone in your life.

By ten o'clock I'd enrolled in the hotel management program at Cornell University, where I'd work my way through in some kitchen. I'd canceled all Mom's credit cards, begun a savings plan for Jazzy's college, and gone through the 7's directory to see what alumni had connections with restaurants, inns, or resorts. . . . I'd talked Dib into going in on the venture with me (even though God knew he'd eat us into the poorhouse), and finally I'd found out Delia's address. For once and for all I'd see her again, one last time, the final period, as Nina'd put it, at the end of the sentence.

At ten thirty I was cold enough to go into rigor mortis, and my normally reliable bladder was blaming me for the coffee I'd brewed back in my room at Sevens and swallowed down on the run.

At twenty minutes to eleven a red taxi from Cottersville Cab stopped in front of the BMW.

I watched while Creery got out. The same long gabardine coat, the Sevens scarf, Timberland boots, and the blue wraparound Gargoyle shades.

He said something to the driver, gave him money, and loped up to number 6. Mark Twain let him in. I saw him smile and clap his arm around Creery's shoulders as he shut the door.

The taxi driver cut the motor and lighted a cigarette.

I counted three more cigarettes smoked and tossed out the window before the driver turned his motor back on, still sitting there, waiting. It was not only freezing cold; there was a wind rising ominously, and I had no doubt that he was tuning in to local radio for the forecast. Snow and gales, followed by blinking digital clocks.

In minutes the snow began dropping in large wet, white flakes. Something dime sized on my back dared me not to itch it. My neck was threatening to lock itself in one position forever. I was starting to sweat, the kind that turns cold and clammy, when I saw the front door at number 6 open.

Creery first . . . then Lauren Lasher appeared.

She was hanging on to him, not because she needed

to, not that way. Because she wanted to. It was all over her eyes.

He was carrying her Le Sac, a big beige thing he had over one arm. Her gloved hand was on the other arm.

She had on a short khaki storm coat with a fur collar, and wide-wale khaki corduroys tucked into boots with thick navy-blue socks tucked over the boot tops. Her long, black hair touched the red scarf tied around her neck.

She was looking up at him. He was looking straight ahead. He didn't look happy. She had the kind of look you have when you're worried about someone you're with. She was talking to him, her lips pursed as though she was saying soothing things.

Then they were telling each other good-bye. Not in words. She had her arms around him. Finally his went around her, too. I couldn't see his face at that moment. Only hers. Her chin nestled in his neck.

He opened the cab door and she got in. He passed the Le Sac to her and gave her a little two-fingered salute, unsmiling, then finally smiling as though she'd said, "Can't you at least smile?" as my mother'd asked me to, at Christmas, when I'd posed for pictures she was taking.

I waited for the cab to take off, and for Creery to go back inside number 6. Then I got out from under and over into the driver's seat.

On Saturdays the buses to Miss Tyler's, in Princeton, left from the Cottersville Inn every three or four hours.

I caught up with the red cab, heading down that way.

Out in front of the inn I caught up with Lauren, honking at her as I pulled over.

She came walking toward the car with a raised eyebrow, shaking her head as though she'd found me out.

I'd been trying to think how I was going to start the conversation, but she started it for me.

"So that was *your* car. Where were you, Fell?"

No way was I going to say under the box.

I said I was "around." I asked her if we could talk.

She said inside, it was too cold, and she had to make a phone call first. She'd meet me in the lobby.

I parked the BMW behind the inn, took care of my bladder in the men's, and waited for her in the lounge.

◘

The Cottersville Inn was where Miss Tyler's girls stayed weekends they attended dances or dated on The Hill. They were always put on the fourth floor, off-limits to any males but uniformed waiters carrying trays.

In the lounge on the first floor the usual Saturday-morning fare was being offered on TV. *Star Trek IV: The Voyage Home.*

A few Miss Tylerites were vaguely involved while they waited for their dates or the school bus back.

Lauren got her coat off and sat down. She had on a red sweater and the gold 7.

"I'm going back on the noon bus," she said, "so there isn't time for you to lie about how you happened to be up on Playwicky Road this morning."

"In time to see that tender farewell between you and Creery," I said. "You're full of surprises, Lauren."

"So are you, Fell. Everyone will know at The Charles Dance anyway. We've been seeing each other. Is that all right with you?"

"If it's all right with you, it's all right with me."

"I hope so. I just talked with Cyr. He thinks Sevens is spying on him. On us. I told him that was your BMW outside. He wants to know what you're after."

"I'm not part of any Sevens team, Lauren."

"Are you the one who found out about us and told Paul?"

"Your brother knew? I didn't realize it was going on that long."

"Cyr and I sneaked around like thieves," she said. "No one over here knew, so we thought. We wrote each other more than we saw each other. Even Daddy didn't know, still doesn't. We met last October. Cyr was someone else's blind date. I took one look at him and that was it."

I tried to imagine what she could have seen in that one look that would make her fall for Creery. His skinhead? The two earrings in one ear? The stoned look in his eyes, like a chicken's staring back at you? Yet she was sitting there admitting it, and wearing his gold, I was sure. Fondling the 7.

"I know what you're thinking," she said, "but Paul talked against Cyr so hatefully, I was expecting this slick con artist, not this shy—"

"Shy?"

"He is, Fell! He's shy and he's sweet. I know he looks goofy, but he's not. He reads Camus and Vonnegut."

"We all read Camus and Vonnegut. They're assigned."

She let that go by.

She said, "Paul and I were very close. Too close. Twins are. We told each other everything. All I used to hear about was Cyr, Paul's great hate. Hearing about someone's great hate is like hearing about someone's great love. You get involved yourself. And curious. When I heard he was coming to our Halloween Dance, I couldn't wait to see him."

Across the room Captain Kirk and Mr. Spock were visiting San Francisco. Behind them the snow was falling so thickly, it was all you could see from the windows.

She seemed to sense my concern about the weather. I was beginning to wonder if I could get the BMW back that afternoon.

"To make a long story short," she said, "at the end of Christmas vacation, Paul told me he knew about us. He said he'd been waiting to see if I'd tell him about it. He said there wasn't a meal he ate all the while we were home that he didn't throw up after. He waited right up until we both had to go back to school, and you know what he said?"

It was one of those questions you weren't expected to answer.

Her face was breaking like a baby's before it starts to cry. "He said . . . Paul said . . . Why didn't you just put a knife in me?"

I waited for her to get ahold of herself.

"So in a way you feel responsible," I murmured.

"Not in a way. I do. Of course I do. . . . We haven't even dared show up on The Hill together. Everyone will think, or *know,* we were the reason for his suicide . . . or they'll wonder how I can date Paul's worst enemy so soon. . . . Cyr's stepbrother says to just face it head-on. Go to The Charles Dance. Deal with it. . . . He's the only one we've confided in until now. . . . Fell? Why were you up on Playwicky today? Is Sevens up to something?"

"No, not Sevens."

I told her about Lasher's letter to Lionel, which had been stored in the word processor. I left out the part about The Sevens Revenge. I explained how Dib had come upon it . . . and how I'd simply gone to Playwicky out of curiosity, after I'd overheard Creery's phone conversation last night.

"I know about Cyr's letter to Lowell," she said. "He wants to get off drugs, Fell. That's all. He wrote Lowell to tell him that, and to tell him about me. I'm helping him straighten out his life. Lowell is too. . . . Why wouldn't The Sevens be glad of that?"

"Maybe Schwartz expected him to do Twilight Truth."

"He might have. But Paul was trying to force it on him!"

"I think there was more in Creery's letter," I said.

"No. Cyr would have told me if there was. . . . And what does it all have to do with *you,* Fell?"

"I'm just nosy, I guess."

"Cyr doesn't believe that. Fell? Why? He's almost flunking out, he's so terrified. Last night he even forgot I was coming on the eight-twenty bus. He can't think straight anymore! And now he's really convinced there's this Sevens Revenge brewing . . . and you could be part of it."

"Tell him I'm not part of anything."

"We don't even know how Paul found out about us. Now you say Paul really did have a copy of Cyr's letter. How did he get it?"

I didn't have any answers for her.

Lauren took out a handkerchief and blew her nose.

She said, "Both Cyr and I are going down the tubes over this thing, Fell. I have to go back to school now and try to study for midsemesters. Cyr's thinking of quitting altogether, and he would, too, if Lowell wasn't there to stop him. You don't *know* how depressed he is! . . . Paul did this!"

"Creery did his share of baiting your brother, too."

"No one is a match for Paul. You don't know him!"

She realized she'd slipped into present tense.

She said, "I mean you didn't know him . . . did you?"

"Not really."

"What he was capable of?"

"I guess not."

Lauren pressed her fingers on my wrist. "I'm going to tell you something that I've only told Cyr and Lowell," she said. "I think Paul picked that fight with Cyr deliberately right before he jumped. He wanted everyone to think Cyr'd pushed him."

There was nothing to say to that.

Lauren looked at her watch. "I have to go, Fell."

I hadn't taken my coat off, only unbuttoned it. I gave another glance out the window and started buttoning it. Someone wrote something that said when it snows hard, the whole world seems composed of one thing and one thing only. That's what it looked like outside.

"There's something I don't understand, though, Lauren," I said. "Why does Creery think The Sevens would want revenge?"

"Do you really want to know what I think? You're not to repeat this to *anyone,* Fell."

"Okay."

"I think trying to come off all the drugs has made Cyr paranoid. Lowell thinks so too. . . . Things are bad enough, but they're not as bad as he's making them." She tapped her forehead. "Up here . . . he needs supervision while he's getting clean."

"Can't this Lowell get him in someplace?"

"Lowell's afraid that if he leaves school now, he'll never go back. His father's dying, too. If he can just hold out four more months!"

I helped her into her coat, and took her Le Sac.

"The lease on the Playwicky apartment is up the first of the month," Lauren said as we walked down the lobby. "Lowell's not going to move into a motel and live here until June."

"Was it just Paul's apartment?"

"Yes. I'd stay there sometimes."

"Because Rinaldo said some of The Sevens used it."

"Only to play cards in. . . . Rinaldo's such a know-it-all, isn't he? I hear he's selling everything we gave him."

"Well . . ." I shrugged.

"I don't care, really. I don't want anything of Paul's! I know right now his ghost is somewhere howling at what he's done to Cyr!"

"I have the material for the memorial book, by the way."

"I finally found a smiling picture of him too. I'll get it to you, and then I wish you'd send it all to Daddy. . . . I don't want to see his sick stories right now."

"Are you going to tell your father about Cyr?"

"I have to . . . and my mother."

Her fingers were back touching the gold 7.

"I'll get the blame for Paul's suicide. From him, not from her." Lauren stopped by the small bus line at the end of the lobby. "My mother would only blame me if it was one of her patients. She only cares about them. She's never even known our shoe sizes."

I handed her the Le Sac.

"I feel a little disloyal to Cyr right now, Fell," she said, "telling you he exaggerates his problems, and I don't believe they're that bad. It doesn't mean that I don't trust him. . . . I want to trust him."

"Yeah," I said. "I know how that works."

I looked through the glass doors at the thickening

snow. It wasn't just the car I wanted to return—I wanted to return to Nina, too.

"Cyr's changing now. I think it's because of me. But you can't become someone new overnight."

"No, you can't," I agreed.

"He doesn't want to be punk anymore . . . or any of it."

"Yes," I said. "There's a time for departure even when there's no certain place to go."

"What an interesting thing to say, Fell."

"It's from *Camino Real,*" I said. "Tennessee Williams wrote it. We had it in English last term."

"But you remembered it," she said. "That's nice."

19

"AMAZING!" Nina said when she opened the door. "Dad's stuck at his office, says he's going across the street to the matinee until the snow stops . . . and Mrs. Whipple's son called to say the roads aren't negotiable."

"They aren't," I said. "What kept me going was the thought of your jar of Fox's U-Bet."

"I thought you were going to say me."

"Don't make me choose between you and an egg cream," I said.

While I took my boots off, Nina took my wet coat and put it on a hanger. Then she hung it on the back of the closet door and put a newspaper under it on the floor.

"If it was anything besides an egg cream, would I have a chance?" she asked me.

I looked up at her while I struggled with my left boot. She had on a black mock-turtle top, black pants, yellow socks, and black lace-up running shoes. Her yellow hair seemed just washed and still damp, no makeup. She was looking better and better to me.

"I'm still mad at you, Nina," I lied.

"Don't be, Fell. I'm a new person."

I made us some egg creams, and we sat in the living room talking. The snow clung to the tree branches winter-wonderland style, while she told me about the new person.

First, the new person was never going to say or think the name Eddie Dragon ever again.

Second, the new person was going to end her analysis.

Third, the new person was going to start shopping for a whole new wardrobe.

"Go back to two," I said. "What does your dad think about that?"

"He's been telling me I ought to take a rest from her. It costs him one hundred and twenty dollars a week. Just imagine all the Easter clothes I can buy! I want to start thinking about outside me for a change. I'm tired of inside me."

"Doesn't Dr. Lasher have a say in that?"

"She'll probably be glad too. She used to complain that I used up her answering machine tapes with all my messages. I'd call and talk as long as I could to her machine, and then I'd just call again and talk, call again and talk. . . . She'd say, Nina, vy can't you vait until de session for all dat?"

The new person was playing Tiffany softly in the background wearing the old person's White Shoulders. I was letting my head rest from thoughts of Lauren and Creery, the letters—all of it—while I watched the snow and her green eyes . . . and thought of Mom as Nina told me how long it had been since she'd gone to the mall.

"Why are you smiling?" she said. "That's part of being a female, caring what you wear, how you look."

"I know it is. But when I'm home, I live with a shopping junkie."

"Who? Your mother or your sister?"

"My sister's only five. It's my mother. My father'd say instead of a gun moll, she was a mall moll."

"What was he like, Fell?"

A personal question from Nina Deem.

I started talking the way someone from Maine basks in the warm sun of July, fearful that it won't last long, that a cold snap is right around the corner.

I think it was close to five o'clock when I was explaining how they "decop" a police officer before he becomes a narc. "Even the posture has to change," I was saying, "because a cop walks with one arm swinging. And another giveaway is not haggling over the price. If the doper says a quarter ounce of pot is fifty, the narc has to talk him down to forty, forty-five. Cops make the mistake of buying anything at any price."

The phone put a stop to my sudden diarrhea of the mouth.

Nina came back from the hall all smiles.

"Dad's met a friend and they're going down the street for dinner. I guess you'll have to cook me mine, Fell. The new person can't think of anything interesting to do with a pair of chicken breasts."

"Where's Meatloaf today?"

"In Dad's office. He has a bed there, and his toys. He has office toys, home toys, and car toys. . . . What happened to Tiffany?"

"My lecture on narcs happened to her," I said. "Do you have any Progresso bread crumbs?"

"You're a brand-name freak, Fell. Do you need them for the chicken?"

"And some Dijon mustard," I said. "They're *my* toys."

⧈

She sat on the stool in the kitchen while I slathered the chicken breasts with Dijon, dipped them in Italian Style Wonder bread crumbs, (not ideal, but okay in a pinch), and dotted them with butter.

"We put them in at four hundred for forty-five minutes," I said.

"That's all there is to it?"

"Wait till you taste them!"

⊡

While we waited, she said she had something to show me.

"It took me a long time to hunt this down," she said, "but the new me is determined to hear you, even if I'm a day late."

She handed me a thin white leather book with THE COTTERSVILLE CLARION written in gold across the front.

"Rinaldo's at the end, in the V's."

I found him immediately. You couldn't miss him. He had the same big, toothy smile, and a certain cock-of-the-walk expression maybe inspired by having good buns and hips that could do things *blancos'* couldn't.

Our Rinaldo on his own turf. He didn't look like somebody you'd send back to the kitchen for a clean fork.

VELEZ, RINALDO A.
"Velly"
Activities: Vice-pres class 2; cheerleader 2, 4;
class treasurer 3; drama 3, 4.
Sports: Tennis, golf, 1, 2, 3, 4

At the bottom of the page there was one of those quotes you found in yearbooks, supposed to sum up someone's personality.

I am
indeed
a king, because I know how to rule myself.
Pietro Aretino

In addition to the formal portrait there was a snapshot of each graduate. Rinaldo's featured him in a magician's cape, pulling a rabbit out of a hat.

The camera angle was bad. Rinaldo was all hands.

I remembered those hands reaching in somewhere else . . . to pull out mail. The blue CORRESPONDENCE box in Deem Library.

I thought of my conversation hours ago with Lauren: *We wrote each other more than we saw each other.* And, of course, I thought of the letter Creery had written to his stepbrother.

What would it have been worth to Lasher to have his own hands on Creery's mail? A pen? A watch? A VCR? Lasher had always believed Creery was involved with drugs and dealing on The Hill.

I handed the book back to Nina.

"There's one other thing about him under Class Prophecy," she said. "They did it in rhyme that year. Here it is."

She read it to me.

"Someday he'll show them on The Hill,
He will!
That he's a match for all of them,
A gem!
Velez, Rinaldo A.
Hooray!"

I wasn't great company at dinner. As soon as the snow stopped, I got ready to hike back.

"Fell," Nina said as she walked me to the door, "when I go to The Charles Dance with you, can I stay in Sevens House overnight like the girls from Miss Tyler's?"

"Your dad won't agree to that."

"Yes, he will. *He* told *me* about it, that they clear a whole floor, and it's the only night girls stay there."

"You'd be stuck in with a lot of other girls, three and four to a room."

"That's what I want, Fell. I want to be like everyone else. I want to have someone say about me what they said about Rinaldo. I want to rule myself."

"If your dad agrees, it's fine with me."

We kissed good-night right before I left.

I wished we hadn't. Either my mind was too much on Rinaldo or my memories were always going to spoil the present. I didn't feel the way I had a summer ago on a beach on Long Island after kissing Delia. I felt more like a preppy on a first date.

⧈

I was definitely down by the time I'd climbed my way through unplowed streets up to The Hill.

I wasn't in the mood for Mrs. Violet and her groupies clustered in the reception room, along with Sevens members and their dates.

It was only around nine o'clock, too early for everyone to be milling around, but I supposed the snow had kept them all from movies and coffeehouses and places they went on Saturday nights.

I knew I should have stopped by the dorm, that by

now Dib would be steamed because I hadn't reported back to him anything that had happened on Playwicky Road.

I also knew I'd earned a Sevens fine of seven dollars for not calling The Tower to say I was skipping dinner.

I tried to make it to the stairs without answering to anyone, when I suddenly saw the familiar blue uniforms.

There were two of them. There are always two.

Then I saw Dr. Skinner, the snow still melting down his bald head, standing in front of the front-hall bulletin board where there seemed to be a space cleared just for him. He had on his mackinaw with a wet scarf, overshoes, standing arms akimbo, reading a sheet of paper thumbtacked there.

There was a semicircle of kids watching him, whispering together.

After he stepped away and walked over toward the policemen, I took his place.

The mystery of the missing letter was solved. There was the copy, for anyone to read.

Dear Lowell,

You will laugh, but can you send me somewhere I can kick this thing?

I mean it, Lowell! I gave myself an early Christmas gift, a new girlfriend. I think the pills are taking over, too. I take more and more and get back less and less.

I know it is my fault you have to work so hard, and I intend to make that up to you. I don't need college. I can learn the business.

This girl, by the way, is the sister of my old enemy, Lasher. Maybe you remember that name. Dad would! She's no dog, either, and I found out I like getting laid better than getting laid back. Did you ever think you'd live to hear me say that?

I don't know how much Dad understands anymore, but tell him not to worry about a Christmas gift for me. He gave me the best when he gave me Sevens. Nothing can top that!

There is Easter break after The Charles Dance, and that would be a good time for me to get clean. It will be the last time you have to pay out for me, Lowell. I promise. There is a place called Oxford Farm outside of Philadelphia. I'll find out more details. It's not just this girl making me determined to get off these pills. She's okay, but the novelty there is she's Lasher's twin and we use his apartment, which would kill him! No, it's more that I've finally grown up. You'll see, Lowell. I know you'll find it hard to believe, but wait! Oxford is supposed to do miracles very fast, too, and I think I could kick this thing in about a week. Come back, graduate, then get my tail down to Miami to become your right-hand man!

Think this over and we'll talk when I'm home. Please save some time.

Yours,
Cyr

Scribbled across the bottom in fresh ink were the words *Self-explanatory . . . Lasher paid for what he found out. Now it's my turn. You'll never see* me *again, either.*

CC

And we didn't. Not alive, anyway.

His body was found in a snowdrift at the bottom of The Tower. His frozen neck was broken from the fall.

20

I AM A SEVENS. *Sevens is part of me as twilight is part of the day, connected and vital to me as the heart to the bloodstream, always and forever.*

I am a Sevens, brother to any Sevens, there for him as the sun and moon are for the tides, always and forever.

"Be seated," said Lionel Schwartz after we recited the oath.

We were in the Sevens House reception room, summoned there through the intercom.

Everyone on The Hill that Sunday morning was dorm or house campused until chapel at eleven.

"At this very moment Dr. Skinner is telling the dorm boys most of what I am going to tell you," Schwartz began, "except for this preamble.

"Before I begin, I call on Fisher to swear us."

Ozzie Fisher stood up. He was the only black Sevens that year. A senior, an ardent political activist when he arrived on The Hill as a junior, he had named his tree for a black hero of South Africa, Mandela.

Some of us were still in our bathrobes. I was. Ozzie was. He stood in front of his chair and waited until The Lion said, "Sevens."

"Richard Wright, Toni Morrison, James Baldwin, Langston Hughes, LeRoi Jones, Gloria Naylor, Countee Cullen."

"Seven black writers, so be it," Schwartz said.

Normally, Schwartz would have given him an argument. The rule of this Sevens ritual was to name seven things that went together, not seven that were alike, but this was not normally, not the occasion to rev up Ozzie's motor. He knew it, and sat down with a glimmer of triumph in his dark eyes.

"This is for Sevens ears only," said Schwartz. "Late Friday evening Cyril Creery came to me and told me he was ready for Twilight Truth, but he hoped meanwhile word would get out that what he had to confess was an accident, and not a deliberate action. As a brother, he would not place me in conflict or jeopardy by giving me information I would be honor bound by Sevens to withold from the authorities, at the same time legally bound to report to them." Schwartz's voice thundered suddenly: "WHY do you think he felt obliged to say that?"

Silence.

"Because," said Schwartz, "of The Sevens Revenge!

He was terrified that we would get to him before he got to us!"

Schwartz peered around the room at all of us through his John Lennon glasses.

"I believe it caused his suicide! . . . I believe he hoped I could prevent this alleged revenge . . . then feared that no one could. The legend of The Sevens Revenge is too overpowering! It overwhelms reason and in the long run it overwhelms justice! That is what it did to Cyril Creery.

"You may say he had no right to be a Sevens, because of his apparent admission that his father told him of the significance of the tree-naming ceremony. BUT . . . he did have a right to Twilight Truth, to speak his piece . . . and where his conflict with Lasher at the top of The Tower is concerned, Cyril Creery had a right to a trial!

"We cannot be anything but ashamed, this morning, that the ugly gossip of The Sevens Revenge forced him to kill himself.

"For once and for all, then, I tell you in this preamble, there is no such thing as The Sevens Revenge! It is a fantasy, a myth, a very dangerous one. Any Sevens who perpetuates it is ultimately destroying Sevens. Remember that."

Then The Lion told us what every boy on The Hill would hear that morning.

1. There would be no memorial service for Cyril Creery. Dr. Skinner opted to deny him such an honor due to his part in Lasher's death.

2. No one on The Hill was to talk with reporters.

3. The police would be investigating. Anyone approached by them was to tell the truth. Sevens would not be expected to explain the Sevens selection process to them, since it was not pertinent to an investigation.

4. The Grief Counselor would be back on campus Monday for individual and group consultation.

5. Everyone on The Hill was to bear in mind that the Gardner Board of Trustees would meet after Easter vacation to vote on the proposal for Gardner to go coed, an idea the student body was resisting. The sooner Gardner was back to normal, the better the chances for Gardner to remain as it was and had been for 123 years.

6. The Charles Dance, a tradition at Gardner for 101 of those years, would take place as scheduled next Saturday evening.

Schwartz took off his spectacles and wiped them clean as he concluded. "This morning, of all mornings, every Sevens member should be present in chapel. . . . We are Sevens . . ."

"Always and forever" came our answer.

The phone call from Lauren Lasher was announced over my intercom just as I had finished knotting my tie.

I put on my suit jacket and went down to the phone booth at the end of the hall, pushing the button that signaled I had picked up.

"Have you sent Paul's writings to my father, Fell?" She started right in, without a hello or any other comment.

"No. We only talked about that yesterday."

"Good! Don't! Daddy doesn't want it mixed in with his other mail. Hang on to it all."

"Lauren, how are you feeling?" I wasn't even sure she knew about Creery's suicide, or the letter he'd posted.

But she knew.

"I'm feeling the same way my family feels," she said. "Very litigious."

"Very *what*?"

"We're going to sue, Fell. That's why I'm calling."

"Are *you* all right?"

"Of course I'm not all right! Someone murders my brother, then tells the world he's screwing me because he hated Paul so much—migawd!"

"It wasn't put exactly that way."

"It's close enough. I read it, Fell."

"Who did you that big favor?"

"It might not sound like a favor, but it was. I have to know, since all of you do. Lowell wasn't in any shape to tell me. He could barely get out the words 'Cyr's dead.' Lionel drove over here last night, and we talked way past lock-in. Miss Tyler's allowed a man downstairs after one A.M. for the first time in its history, I guess. . . . I'm a mess, so don't smart mouth me, Fell."

"I had no intentions of—"

She cut me off. She wasn't in any mood for small talk.

"We figured out Cyr probably found a way to let Paul know about us, since that was his main interest: getting even with Paul."

"And how did your brother get Cyr's letter?"

"The way Cyr suspected, probably: went into his room, found the copy."

"I'm not so sure."

"Fell? Do me a favor, hmmm? Stop being boy detective. I don't care, at this point, how Paul got the letter. I don't care about any of the little cow pies you might come upon. It's enough for me to know about the cow. Do you get my meaning?'

"Yes. I'll cork it."

"Thanks. . . . I'm going to The Charles Dance with Schwartz."

"How come?"

"He said Paul would have wanted The Sevens to give me support. He said the sooner I faced people, the better it would be for me."

"Well, that's probably true, Lauren."

"Or maybe he just suspects my family will hold Gardner *and* Sevens liable for Paul's murder. . . . Maybe he's trying to soften me up."

"No. It sounds like something Schwartz would think to do. He's very conscientious and thoughtful."

"I don't trust anyone at this point."

"That's understandable."

"Stop being so agreeable! I hate all of you right now!'

"Okay."

"Maybe not you. Sorry, Fell. . . . Something else. I hope you saved the microwafer with Paul's letter to Schwartz on it."

"Yeah."

"Naturally Schwartz claims he never got the letters, didn't know anything about them, doubts Paul put them in his box. We need Paul's as evidence."

"Evidence for what, Lauren?"

"It proves Cyr really had reason to kill Paul, and that Sevens knew he did . . . or Schwartz knew it, anyway."

"Maybe your brother never printed it out. He'd been stalling since Christmas."

"You don't believe that, and neither do I!"

"Why would Schwartz lie?"

"Because he's protecting Sevens, Fell! He puts Sevens before any other consideration! He was probably conferring with other Sevens to try and decide what to do, how to handle it! . . . Daddy says that little delay is going to cost them!"

Where had the simple life gone? Days I'd only have to worry about Keats playing around behind my back, my mother loose with her credit card in some shopping center, Delia's soft smile lying lovingly into my naive eyes, small, everyday occurrences in the life of a growing boy? Not homicide, suicide, and now litigiousness in preppydom.

I could hear the chapel bells tolling.

"Lauren? I have to go now, but before I do—I'm sorry all this had to happen."

"Some of it didn't *have* to happen. Cyr didn't have to put that letter up on the bulletin board for the whole world to see! Damn him! If he wasn't dead, I'd—"

I could hear the sob.

"Yeah," I said. "I'm sorry, Lauren."

"We're still going to do the memorial book, grim as Paul's writings were. Mother thinks it's like Jungian synchronicity, that he probably had a premonition of his early death. . . . We'll talk at The Charles Dance, Fell. You'll have time, won't you?"

"I'll make time."

"Because we want to go ahead as soon as possible. Paul would have wanted vindication. Nobody at that school cared but you and that Dibble kid! You and he and Daddy were the only ones who gave Paul the benefit of the doubt!"

"There're still some unanswered questions," I said.

"FELL?" she said threateningly.

"Okay," I said. "Okay."

⧈

But after chapel I *did* take care of one last loose end.

⧈

First, I tried to get Dib inside and make a date to talk. I hurried out of chapel after him. He waved me away and jumped into the old Mustang with Little Jack at the wheel. It was parked just a few cars behind Dr. Skinner's long, black limousine.

I walked down to The Tower by myself then, the cold winter sun warming me. I couldn't help think of Creery, seeing his face in my memory ways I'd never viewed it before. Sad ways of seeing the vacant eyes and silly punk paraphernalia. Alive, he'd angered me, reminding me of an old self maybe still around somewhere inside me . . . but dead, no longer any kind of threat to me, he made me think only of the waste, and how he wrote his stepbrother: *I think I can kick this thing.* . . . I thought of the dumb idea he had that he could be clean in just a week . . . and the stupid bravado bragging about having Lauren, getting laid . . . all the very personal things a guy could write, *I* could have written, never thinking it would get into someone's hands it wasn't meant for.

Rinaldo was in the kitchen, and the smell of rib roast wafted from inside as I called through the door.

While I waited for him in the empty library, I thought of the fear of The Sevens Revenge that Schwartz had spoken about that morning.

Maybe Lasher had delayed giving Schwartz those letters purposely, to feed that fear in Creery. Maybe Lasher had known The Revenge was fictitious but counted on the idea Creery would be left to wait for The Sevens to act . . . and the longer the wait, the worse the imagining of what would be done to him.

I could still picture Creery with the little rat tail behind his head, running around in his long gabardine coat and his Timberland boots.

Death brought it all back and colored it in softer hues, so even Creery seemed more human dead, and I felt differently about him. Sorry or something. But I felt for him, and it surprised me.

So did Rinaldo surprise me, coming up suddenly behind me, his hand over my eyes.

"Guess who?"

I took a chance while he was grinning down at me. "Lasher left something in the word processor about how he got Creery's letter to his stepbrother."

Rinaldo pulled out a chair. "Can I sit?"

I shook my head.

"And how he found out about Creery and Lauren."

"What do you want, Fell?" He wasn't grinning any longer.

"You took the mail from the CORRESPONDENCE box every night," I said. "One of Creery's letters for a watch? That was a fair price."

"Now you're going to try and do blackmail, Fell?"

"No blackmail. . . . Another letter, a pen. Right, Rinaldo?"

"I don't play the twilight game. That's for you guys."

"Just tell me about the mail game. I promise you it's just for my information."

"I gave him nothing, and if he wrote I did, he's lying."

"But he got into the mail."

"I turned my back and he got into the mail. He was looking for a way to connect Creery with dope, and he found a different connection. The sister. That ate at him until just before Christmas. Then the letter to the stepbrother was like butter on a burn. I knew from his reaction he'd struck gold. But I never saw any one of the letters, not one. He copied them on the Xerox machine over there. I never touched a letter, never handed one to him. . . . He showed up the last thing at night when I came here to unlock the box. I turned my back."

"And accepted payment."

"No money."

"I'm not saying you took money."

"I made an error in judgment, yes I did. He knew my weakness: nice things I could never afford. I learned to like those things from Sevens. Everything but your taste in clothes. I live surrounded by the good life."

"How many Sevens have Gstaad watches and apartments in town?"

"You know what I mean, Fell. You all live like you have them. I am part of Sevens, and I'm not. I have my steak on Wednesday nights, but I eat it in the kitchen on a stool. You get a chance to eat at the table for once, you take it."

We could hear other Sevens arriving at The Tower for Sunday lunch.

"I know Creery suspected me too. Maybe he didn't know I let Lasher see the mail, but he believed Lasher told me things that Lasher never would. So-o-o—" He turned up his palms. "I was afraid too, for a while. I thought always that Creery killed him. We were the only ones here that day. I was sure of that. . . . Can you erase this thing in that machine?"

"There isn't anything about it in there. It was just my hunch, Rinaldo."

Outside, in the hall, Outerbridge was singing the hymn he'd sung in chapel.

"Ride on! ride on in majesty!
In lowly pomp ride on to die."

Rinaldo stood up, "I don't fear you, Fell. Warn me if I should. . . . I have always feared your curiosity, but not you. You have not been in Sevens long enough for that."

He didn't wait for reassurance.

And I was thinking back to a day on Long Island when a stranger offered to pay my way to go to Gardner, posing as his son. It was how I'd gotten there. My own chance to eat at the table. Never mind all the foul-ups that had come as result—I'd made quite a trade, too, for a better life.

21

THE AFTERNOON OF The Charles Dance, I felt as though I was carrying Nina's entire closet when I lugged her garment bag into Sevens House. She said I wasn't that far wrong. She'd brought a lot of changes, because she wanted options in case things she tried on looked awful.

"At home I always change at least three times before I go anywhere important. Do boys?"

"Not boys going to The Charles Dance. One costume is enough."

I'd already rounded up a handlebar mustache and a monocle, to go as Damon Charles. The rest was easy: a rented tux and a pair of evening shoes borrowed from Dib.

He wasn't going. He was dorm campused. Last Sunday Little Jack had been pulled over for drunken driving. He and Dib had spent Sunday afternoon in Cottersville Tavern. Dib wasn't charged with anything, claimed he hadn't been drinking. But the place was off-limits to Hill boys, so Dr. Skinner decided, finally, to suspend Dib's privileges.

We were on the kind of speaking terms that just barely spoke. When he got the dusty pumps out of the bottom of his closet, he threw them at me. I wanted to apologize for not calling him from Nina's, after I'd left Playwicky that morning, but he gave me the finger.

"Cork it, Fell! You got what you came for! Take them and get back to your Sevens!"

"We've got to talk sometime, Dib."

"About what? How wonderful you are?"

"Let's talk about how wonderful Little Jack is!" I said. I could see a Charlie Chaplin costume in the rental box on his desk, the cane and derby on top.

He saw me look that way, and he snapped, "Little Jack did me a favor! I'm not into kids' parties. You guys ought to grow up!"

I took the damn shoes. Then I was out of there.

I'd managed to get Nina assigned to my room, with Outerbridge's sister and Kidder's date, while I bunked downstairs, dorm style, with six other Sevens.

When I met Nina in the reception room that night, I was glad girls couldn't wear costumes. She was a knockout in an ankle-length white silk dress, hiding the blue-winged dragonfly but leaving her arms and back bare.

She had on white sling-back shoes that made winter seem like June, and made her look like a bride.

She was nervous and excited. I helped her into her coat.

"Let's not say anything on the way there, Fell. I'm too hyper."

I said okay with me, slipped the monocle into my pocket, and put on the blue half mask all Sevens wore until intermission.

It was about fourteen degrees out, but we didn't have far to go. The walk to the gym was clear; so was the weather. There was a slipper moon rising. I wished Mom could see us. I'd called her that morning. She had a job as hostess in a restaurant at the World Trade Center; she wasn't due there until noon.

"You never told me if you liked the gold 7," I'd said.

"I called you and got Mrs. Violet. You never called back."

"You don't like it, hmmmm?"

"I like it well enough, Johnny. Of course, our apartment number's seven, and I feel like some old lady who's wearing something that'll tell the neighbors where she lives if she's found running around the neighborhood babbling."

"I thought you'd like it."

"I do. I'm going to get some head charms to hang on it—a boy's head for you and a girl's for Jazzy. Macy's will engrave names on them."

Mom never wore one of anything except her wedding ring.

She said, "People are always asking me what's 7 mean."

"Well? Do you tell them?"

"What can I tell them? I've got a son in some club I don't even know how he got into?" She laughed. "I tell them it's in case I forget how many days there are in the week."

Jazzy got on the phone to tell me her favorite doll, Georgette, was in love with a doll named Mr. Mysterious, who wore a mask, cost $32.75, and could be purchased at most shopping malls.

In the background I could hear the fashion channel on television. A woman's voice was describing a polka-dot sun dress with a bolero top and spaghetti straps underneath.

"Johnny?" Mom said when she got back on. "Are you meeting any nice girls?"

"I've met one named Nina."

"I hope she's not your usual type."

"What's my usual type, Mom?"

"Someone who can run circles around you. Someone who's older and wiser, like that Keats person."

Even Mom knew better than to mention Delia.

"This Nina person isn't like that Keats person," I said.

"Watch out, Johnny! You're a cream puff when it comes to the ladies!"

At the dance I'd nab the photographer and have a picture taken for Mom. One look at Nina in all white, and Mom would start fantasizing the wedding, the house we'd all move into, and the grandchildren she could buy more head charms for at Macy's.

I spared Mom the news about Creery, just as I had the Lasher story. The *Cottersville Compass* was already hinting that a suicide on The Hill was purportedly tied into the death earlier of another student. I didn't know how long it would take the news services to pick it up, or if Mom would even see it when they did. She probably wouldn't unless it was on the same page announcing a white sale or 50% Off Everything.

On the phone that week, I'd told Nina what I knew.

"Boy, does my shrink have egg on her face!" she'd said, the moment we'd sped away from her house in the BMW Mr. Deem had lent me. "Her groat-hormone theory was shot all to pieces!"

"Did she say anything Thursday?"

"I told you, Fell. I quit. Dad calls it a hiatus, but it's over. From now on I'm on my own."

She was, too. Or *I* was. As soon as we started dancing, the stag line began descending on us.

I lost her to Charlie Chan, Charles Dickens, Charles Bronson, three or four of the Charlie Chaplins who were there in force, and Charlie Chan again.

I began to feel as though I was ready for grief counseling with HEADOC, whose red Maserati had been in the faculty parking lot all week.

There was a seven-piece band playing, blue-and-white 7's hanging from the ceiling, where seven golden angels swung from fluffy clouds in Seventh Heaven. (It had seemed like a good idea when we were planning the decorations, but there was something slightly macabre about it in view of Creery's death . . . or maybe I'd just spent too much time reading Lasher's writings about heaven.)

The seven chaperones wore white dresses or blue suits.

"Fell?" Nina said at one point, when I'd wrenched Charlie Chan's white-gloved hands from her shoulder a third time. "If I don't remember to thank you for this, thank you now."

She put her fingers up on my cheek lightly, and we looked at one another for maybe six seconds. That was all it took for me to see the wisdom and the heartbreak of chaperones and separate quarters for overnight visitors.

Some of Charlie Chan's greasepaint had come off on Nina's dress.

"Thank heavens I brought a change, Fell!" she said to me at intermission. "Look at me!"

We were heading to Sevens House for the intermission ceremony. Mrs. Violet presided over the punchbowl there, while dorm boys served their dates from the bowl in the gym.

This was the time when The Sevens unmasked. The lights went off in the reception room, and our faces were illuminated by tiny gold flashlights shaped like 7's, CHARLES engraved down their sides. Each girl was given a corsage of white roses and blue ribbons, and most kept their dates' flashlights as souvenirs.

For the first time I saw Lauren and The Lion. He was in seventeenth-century costume as Charles II of England.

"That's my shrink's daughter, isn't it?" said Nina. "She looks enough like her to make me shake! . . . Let me go up and change before I meet her!"

⊡

"Nina *who*?" Lauren asked me after I explained my date was "freshening up," and as The Lion strutted down to the john.

"Deem. Nina Deem."

"Oh, *Fell!* How did you get roped into that?"

She passed me an envelope marked *Photograph. Paul, sometime last autumn.*

"Wait till you see her!" I said.

Lauren was in a red wool dress, her hair pulled up on her head, pearls dangling down the front. Red shoes. The smell of Obsession.

"That's the smiling picture of Paul," she said.

I was getting it out of the envelope.

"I know Nina Deem," said Lauren. "She was mother's client. Past tense, so I can tell you watch out for her, Fell. She's needy. And that's a *nice* way to put it."

"I like her. You will, too."

"Fell, she'd get on my mother's answering machine and use up all the tape whining about this married dope pusher she had a crush on. Of course, *she* claimed he'd been framed. She was obsessed with what his wife was like, *convinced* he didn't love her. She'd go on and on about him, on the tape! Paul and I called her Screaming

Nina. When we were home, we'd tune in to her and howl!"

I pulled Lauren to one side, away from the punch and the girls in the gowns with their Charleses.

"Tell me more, Lauren. She *knew* he was married?"

"She knew, all right. She was dying to get a look at his wife. I hope you're not involved, Fell!"

"What else?"

I was holding the photograph of Lasher in my hands while I listened.

"*Are* you involved with Screaming Nina?"

I hardly heard the question. I was looking at the picture of her brother. Lasher was dressed up in a gay-nineties costume, sitting on a bench, the waterfall, the old mill, the weeping willow behind him.

"This was taken at Dragonland," I said.

"I don't know where it was taken. It was in a thingamajig and I pulled it out, because look at him smile! Paul never smiled unless he was up to something."

"Then he knew Eddie Dragon," I said.

Lauren looked at me. "That's the name of Screaming Nina's boyfriend," she said. "How would Paul have known him?"

I didn't answer Lauren, not only because I didn't have an answer but also because of what I saw suddenly across the room.

Charlie Chan was leaving Sevens House, putting on his coat over his costume, his gloves off, and there was something on his wrist I'd seen before. A dragonfly.

I started running, down the hall and up the stairs,

the voice of The Sevens shouting after me "Off-limits to males tonight!"

Someone grabbed my coattails to stop me.

Kidder.

"Your date's not up there, Fell. She just went out the side door."

22

I GOT OUT in the parking lot in time to see them take off in a white Isuzu jeep.

Nina hadn't changed clothes. I could see her pulling her coat around the white dress. She must have used the time to lug her garment bag down to his car.

I didn't have the BMW keys with me, but I remembered Mr. Deem telling me about the spare in the ashtray.

I got in fast and went after them, picking the jeep up in my headlights near the traffic light at the top of the hill.

They made a left, heading into Cottersville, and I followed a few car lengths behind them.

My mind was spinning like the BMW's wheels: recalling how Nina'd said she'd begged her father to let her go to The Charles Dance . . . then how she'd come up soon after with the idea to stay overnight. I thought of Nina telling me she'd brought a lot of changes in her garment bag, and I remembered the way she'd thanked me for the evening right before intermission.

And of course I was remembering the afternoon at Dragonland, the way she'd pretended to be shocked by the idea Eddie was married. She'd known that all along, used me to satisfy her curiosity about Ann Dragon.

Lauren had laughed at the idea Nina'd claimed Eddie didn't love his wife. But my money was on Nina.

I was learning the hard way: Nina didn't *get* surprised as much as she surprised. And calculated. Nina went after what she wanted, even if it involved flirting her way along and giving little innocent-sounding speeches about how she was going to learn to take control of her life.

She didn't need any lessons in that.

What had Nina said to her father that first night I'd had dinner there? Something about the word "elope," after Mr. Deem said it was a word we didn't hear much anymore. Those who have a reason to use it do, Nina had said.

In Cottersville I inched up until I was right behind them.

Dragon wasn't doing any fancy driving. He was keeping to the forty-mile limit, heading out toward the shopping center.

What I couldn't figure out was how Lasher fit into the puzzle, what he was doing at Dragonland last fall.

I pushed the heat up all the way. They had coats, I

didn't. I had an idea I wouldn't be getting out of the BMW for a long time, anyway . . . and that as soon as we hit the highway past the mall, I'd be in a race.

That was where I was wrong.

The Isuzu pulled into the shopping center's large lot, almost empty at that hour.

I followed.

Dragon headed toward the only parked car down in front of the Food Basket. It was a black Pontiac, its lights beaming up suddenly as the jeep came near it.

Then Dragon stopped.

When I pulled up, Dragon got out and stood there waiting for me. He'd ripped off his mustache and the rubber skin from his head. His hair was blowing in the wind, face streaked with greasepaint.

As I cut my motor, I saw the gun pointed at me.

That was when the driver of the Pontiac got out too, crossing to the jeep, reaching to help Nina with the garment bag she'd pulled out onto the asphalt.

It was Ann Dragon.

I could see Nina's face, tears streaming down it, while Ann led her toward the Pontiac.

"Get in the jeep!" said Eddie Dragon.

23

HE WAITED while Ann Dragon got Nina into the front seat of the Pontiac and the garment bag into the back.

I could see the dragonfly tattoo very clearly now as his left hand gripped the steering wheel, while his right one kept the gun trained on me.

"Have you moved from dope into kidnaping now?" I said.

"Just shut up!"

The Pontiac took off.

He turned back to me, swiveling his shoulders so he could look me in the eyes.

"My name is Ted Draggart. I'm an FBI undercover man. You're who? Somebody Fell?"

"John Fell. And I don't believe you. FBI men don't have tattoos."

"I'm doing the talking right now, John! . . . Nina is not being kidnaped, and you don't know shit about FBI men! . . . Nina is with my partner. We've been undercover here for almost a year. Ann will take Nina someplace safe, while you come with me. Do you understand?"

"Why doesn't Ann just take Nina home?"

"Because that's where *we're* going. I didn't count on you, but now that you're here, I'm going to have to! You're going to have to count on me if you want to save your ass, so start trusting me."

I didn't say anything, just watched while he stuck the gun in the top of his pants.

He started the jeep.

"I'll fill you in as much as I can, so you'll understand the action. For God's sake get rid of the handlebars!"

I'd forgotten my mustache, and I tore it off.

"You paid a visit to the base we set up. Dragonland." He started the jeep. "Everyone paid a visit there but the ones we expected."

"Nina. Me . . . Paul Lasher."

He snorted. "Yeah. Paul Lasher. When you're dredging, you get the dregs. But he was a bonus, it turned out. Let me tell you a few more things before we come to Lasher."

We were heading back to Cottersville.

He said, "Ann and I were given a name."

"She's your wife."

"She's my partner. Let *me* talk, John. . . . The name was David Deem. We got it from a fairly reliable source, if you want to call someone with dope connections and convictions reliable. But he wanted to make a deal, get himself out of serving twenty years. Deem was the bite. Our informer knew there was a sporting-goods setup involved too, but nothing else. . . . Ann and I set ourselves up in Point Pleasant after we got a read on Deem. Our case agent had nothing to incriminate Deem, so we came in blind."

We were making all the right turns that would take us to Jericho Road.

"I angled to meet Nina," Dragon said. "We'd found

out she was the only one he had left to care about. She was my 'in' to Deem. I met him, and I found out all I could, which wasn't much. . . . Later we fixed my arrest for selling cocaine and arranged to get me off, with the newspapers picking up the story. . . . We didn't figure Deem himself would come after me. Everything we knew about him was clouded over, anyway, but we figured him as a guy who wouldn't want anyone muscling in on his territory . . . and particularly his daughter. We thought he'd send someone to Dragonland to threaten me, someone who'd lead us to his operation by some zigzag route."

"Deem sells drugs?"

"Not exactly. Not at all what we thought. Deem doesn't have a territory. He's a facilitator. He doesn't sell anything; he helps it get sold. He has this mail-order deal called DOT. Short for Deem Out There. Advertises: Out There You'll Need Us. All-weather equipment. Let me finish, John," he said, as I started to tell him I'd heard Nina mention DOT. "There isn't time now." He looked at his watch and picked up some speed.

"Your friend Lasher—"

"He wasn't my friend."

"This Lasher came to Dragonland last fall. He'd read the newspaper write-up of my arrest. He was sniffing around, trying to see if I knew this Creery. There was a point when I even thought he was trying to frame Creery, or get him killed. I didn't have time for it, didn't want him around, but while he was there he said he knew a lot about my girlfriend, Nina Deem.

"I paid attention suddenly. I asked him how the hell he knew her name. He told me his mother was her shrink. Then he began playing the bigshot, telling me a lot of stuff about Nina, like the fact I'd told her I was married. I finally told her that after my arrest. She'd gotten herself a tattoo like mine over in Lambertville. That's the first I realized she'd made this thing into a big romance."

"She fell in love with you. Didn't you *angle* for that?"

"She was a kid! I thought she had a crush on me, sure, but I never encouraged it, never even held her hand—nothing! I didn't count on this flood of emotion. She'd call Dragonland even after I told her not to, to let *me* get in touch with *her*. Then she appeared with you. And after that she called to apologize for bringing you there. I couldn't discourage the contact with her altogether, because I needed that."

We were passing Main Pharmacy and Playwicky Road.

Dragon said, "You see, Lasher let something drop that got my ears pricking. He said his mother told him Nina was going away at Easter. It was going to be a surprise. Her father was planning to take her to Europe. . . . Lasher said maybe I could use that information . . . and maybe he could get me more if I'd help him get this Creery. . . . I wanted him to go because he was just in the way. I told him I didn't want to run off with Nina, thanks anyway, I was happily married. I had a hell of a time getting him out of there that day. He hung around, had his picture taken. . . . But he'd given me the tip: Deem was going to run in March. We had to work fast!"

We were a block from Jericho.

Dragon was slowing up. He said, "A few months later Lasher was killed. . . . I sent in for information on this Creery. Routine, not my province, but Lasher'd said Creery used drugs, so you never know. . . . I asked for anything the computer had on Creery, and lo and behold, we found a connection to DOT. It was there all along, but we hadn't been looking for it, and it still isn't too clear. I tried to get a court order to tap Deem's phone. It never came through, and we found out Deem was booked to go this Sunday. . . . We're going to park a few doors away. My backup's there somewhere. John, I don't want you to leave this car, okay?"

"Yes." It was beginning to fit, all of it. I knew then why Mr. Deem was so eager to get Nina to The Charles Dance that weekend, and why he'd allowed her to stay overnight. He was making all the arrangements in the house, packing up, preparing to close it and clear out.

I said, "And I suppose Nina thought you were eloping with her tonight!"

"She probably did, but there was no other way. When she told me she could stay overnight on The Hill, I was afraid Deem might take off solo. . . . Maybe not, but we couldn't take that chance, so we moved. We put a man on Jericho while Ann and I went for Nina. I wanted her out of there, and I wanted her prepared for what she's going to have to find out about her father. Ann's taking her in, and telling her everything. She'll be good with her, John."

"Fell," I said.

"Fell. I care a lot about Nina too."

We went down Jericho and parked two doors away from the house.

We weren't there long before a man rapped on my window.

Eddie Dragon said, "You sit tight, Fell."

He got out.

I heard him say he had a Hill boy with him who'd stay in the jeep. I watched him stop and drop something. Then he turned around and came back to the passenger side.

The man was right behind him.

I rolled down my window.

"I didn't count on this, Fell. Sorry." Dragon said.

"No conversations!" a voice barked. "Just get him out and in the house!"

It wasn't a voice I'd ever heard before, but I knew the face when I saw it.

Mark Twain from Miami.

He was stopping to pick up Dragon's gun from the street. Then he had two.

24

THE PHONE WIRES were cut, Deem told me, and there was a naked man locked in the crawl space. Deem said he had no idea who the man was, that Meatloaf had been let out to do his business and routed him out of the bushes. Then Hunter had taken his clothes, to go through them and to limit his action.

We were locked in, too, Deem and I, in Deem's study. If we tried anything, Hunter'd warned us, he'd kill us both.

From the sounds below, Dragon was being put in with the backup.

"At least Nina's safe," I said.

"No she isn't. Hunter made me call the school and say she was to come home immediately, alone. He sent a taxi for her."

I explained that she was with Ann, that Dragon had seen to that. Then I told him who Dragon was, or what he was . . . that Ann was his partner, and the naked man part of their team.

He looked too frightened to understand what I'd told him. "Don't try anything, Fell," he said. "Hunter means it when he says he'll kill us."

He was sitting in his big Eames chair hugging Meatloaf.

"What could I try? There're bars on those windows."

I was still absorbing the idea this man was involved

with dope. He looked the same to me, right down to the suit, the necktie, and the shine on his shoes. It was hard for me to imagine him jaywalking, much less "facilitating" drug sales.

He knew I'd been told something by Dragon. He was having trouble looking at me, though I was right there on his footstool. It was the first time we'd ever been face to face when I'd had shoes on.

"Hunter killed his own stepbrother," he said finally. "Now he's going to kill me, too."

"How do you know he killed Creery, sir?" I didn't mean to call him "sir," but habit won out. He seemed to respond to the respect I'd given him unintentionally, and he met my eyes for the first time.

"I suspected as much," he said, "and when I accused him of it tonight, he told me he'd kill Nina, too, if I didn't cooperate with him. . . . What have I done, Fell?" he sighed. "What *have* I done?"

"How did you ever get involved with someone like Hunter?" I said. He had a handkerchief out and was mopping his brow.

He said, "You might as well hear it from me, Fell. Tell Nina, too; otherwise she'll never learn the truth. I won't live to tell her."

He lifted Meatloaf up to his chest and held him hard. "A long time ago, Bob Creery and I had dinner one night in Miami. We'd been friends in Sevens. My business was bad. He said he could help me out." He leaned down and brushed his lips against the top of the dog's head. "Bob was sort of an entrepreneur. That's a polite name for it. He had his paint business in Miami, a couple of warehouses. He was sometimes legitimate, mostly not. Bootleg stuff. We formed DOT together. I sold stolen goods. . . . It wasn't right, of course, but no one got hurt. Insurance covered the losses. . . . That was the way I rationalized it. DOT thrived. So did I. . . . Oh, Fell, Sevens did something to me. It gave me a taste for certain comforts, small luxuries. I'd never been as happy as when I lived as a Sevens. . . . I got spoiled for any kind of life that wouldn't be easy."

Meatloaf jumped out of his lap and down to my feet to sniff me.

Deem said. "Everything turned sour right before Barbara died. Bob had his stroke, and his stepson couldn't wait to take over! Next thing I knew we were in the cocaine business. It was being shipped from South America to the paint factory inside croquet mallets, the handles of tennis racquets, anything wooden. It holds up well in wood and doesn't add that much extra weight. . . . He sent me samples to show me until I said, 'I don't want to know about it—stop it.' He'd empty out the cocaine, paint the stuff, and ship it on. My equipment and DOT gave him another outlet. He's got outlets all over the country."

"Did Creery's father know, or Creery?"

"Bob wouldn't have allowed it, not Bob. He wasn't a man of any integrity, but he wouldn't have okayed drug trafficking. . . . It's too dirty . . . and it's too risky. I wouldn't have either, if Hunter hadn't known all about DOT. Bob was paralyzed all down one side, and that left me at Hunter's mercy." Deem folded his handkerchief neatly and placed it carefully back in his breast pocket. "The boy didn't know, I'm sure. Hunter pretended to get the kid off pot by substituting pills. That's why there were rumors that Cyril was selling, because he could get all he wanted. Of course the kid got hooked. Hunter wanted him addicted. But that boy thought it was his own fault he couldn't stop. . . . And he was being bullied by that Lasher boy."

"Well . . . they bullied each other."

"I think he taunted him once too often. Didn't Nina say he had proof of some kind that Bob told him how to get into Sevens?"

"Yes. There was a letter."

"I believe the story going around The Hill that Cyril killed Lasher. An associate of Hunter's told me, just last fall, that the boy was on a combination of amphetamines and Quaaludes. There was plenty of Miami gossip regarding young Cyril, speculation about how Hunter'd deal with him after Bob's death. . . . And drugs change your whole personality. You live a nightmare. You love the drug more than you love anything. Well"—he gave a strange little choked cough—"that's how we got rich. Cocaine made us rich. Richer than we'd ever been. . . . Hunter is a greedy man, Fell. He wanted that little empire for himself. Bob's near death. Cyril would have inherited everything from Bob . . . and there'd be a lot of explaining to do. So Hunter saw his chance."

"But if he knew Creery'd killed Lasher, why didn't he just turn him in?"

Deem shook his head. "No. In our business we know too well how elastic the law is. Hunter didn't want Cyril alive. The law wouldn't kill him, so Hunter did. . . . I didn't even know he was up north until Cyril was found dead. We never made phone calls to each other. We met in Florida, always. We never wanted any record of rapport. . . . Even after young Cyril's death, I never expected him to walk through that door the way he did tonight. . . . Walked in here and caught me red-handed, said, You're not going anywhere. . . . Poor Nina. My poor, poor Nina."

I picked Meatloaf up and handed him to Deem. He needed to hold on to something, do something with his hands, which he'd begun to wring. I'd never make a good policeman. I felt too sorry for people I knew who got themselves into trouble. I could see myself in them, maybe, see how easy it was to start heading down the wrong road.

"They say it's a small world." Deem was talking into Meatloaf's neck. "And it is indeed. Do you know how Hunter learned I was planning to bolt?"

He didn't wait for my answer.

He said, "Hunter spent some time with Inge Lasher's daughter these past few weeks. She told him her brother thought a man named Eddie Dragon was supplying Cyril with the pills. Cyril'd never told her the truth. . . . Then she told Hunter about Nina being mixed up with Dragon: She'd heard her on the answering machine. . . . One day Dr. Inge told her, Don't worry, she won't be calling here after Easter, Mr. Deem is taking her away. . . . Well. That was all Hunter needed to hear. He did a little investigating on his own, called the travel bureau, and found out I was leaving tomorrow morning."

"Thank God for Eddie Dragon," I said. "Or whatever his real name is. He got Nina out, anyway."

"He started it all," Deem said bitterly.

I noticed Deem blamed everyone but himself. Sevens. Hunter. Eddie Dragon.

"By now Hunter knows he's trapped, too. He can't lock up the whole Cottersville police force in the dry cellar, can he? They'll be along, won't they?" He seemed ready to cry. "I hope you'll be kind enough to take care of Meatloaf, Fell. And to tell Nina I truly love her. . . . Hunter won't hurt you. Just me. I never should have put bars on those windows."

I was praying that he was right about the police coming, that by then Ann had gotten to them. But I was also remembering my father telling me of times local police didn't interfere with federal arrests.

We didn't say any more for a while. Deem sat there cradling Meatloaf in his arms like a baby. Then we heard a door slam.

Meatloaf began barking. "Don't, darling," Deem told the dog. "Hush and don't make trouble." He put his thumb and finger over Meatloaf's nose like a muzzle.

Hunter unlocked the study door and appeared with an armful of clothes, a gun peeking out from under trousers and shirts, underpants, coats, and shoes.

"I'll take your car keys, David," he said.

I petted Meatloaf with trembling hands. He was making low sounds close to growling. The gun in Hunter's hand was aimed at me and the dachshund.

The dog jumped down as Deem reached into his pocket.

Hunter looked at me and said, "You're coming!"

"Why take the boy?" Deem asked.

"For a shield," Hunter said.

Deem dropped the keys into Hunter's palm.

At first when I heard the noise, I thought there was a radio on in the house.

Then, as it became louder, I knew what it was.

"What the hell is that?" Hunter snapped.

He walked over to the window.

I could see the look on his face, and I knew I'd always remember it. The flesh caved in, and the eyes got wide.

"Get over here!" he said to me. "What the hell is this?"

They were in the yard with their gold flashlights shining on their faces. Singing.

I could see Charles Dickens and Charles II, Charles Bronson and two Charlie Chaplins.

There were about a dozen Sevens there. Kidder I recognized, and Fisher. Schwartz next to Fisher.

They were in good voice and I'd never felt more like joining in.

The time will come as the years go by,
When my heart will thrill
At the thought of The Hill,

And the Sevens who came
With their bold cry,
WELCOME TO SEVENS!

Then they began to shout our names, seven times apiece.

"DEEM! DEEM! DEEM! DEEM! DEEM! DEEM! DEEM!"

Behind me Meatloaf was dancing to the door and barking.

"Shut that damn dog up!" Hunter cried out.

There were tears rolling down Deem's cheeks as he realized they'd come to rescue him, however they had gotten word he needed them.

I might have bawled myself, but I had gone to quiet Meatloaf, near the door, telling him to be still, a moment before my hand reached for the knob and my legs did the rest.

I had my own cheering section to spur me on.

"FELL! FELL! FELL! FELL! FELL!"—and I was out of there for the last two.

25

WHEN THE COTTERSVILLE POLICE arrived in their car, Dr. Skinner pulled up in the Gardner limo.

I told one cop about the naked men in the crawl space while another began calling to Deem and Lowell Hunter through a bullhorn, advising them that the house was surrounded, to come out hands up.

"I want you and Schwartz to come with me, Fell," Skinner said to me.

"Can't we wait to see them come out?"

"No. We're going back to The Hill with Lieutenant Hatch. He's going to ask some questions, and I hope he's going to answer some. . . . Schwartz had better answer some too—about how Sevens got dragged into this!"

Skinner went over and tapped Schwartz on the shoulder.

I could hear Schwartz tell him he'd go back in Kidder's van with the other Sevens. But Skinner shook his head no. He pointed to the limo.

"Right now?" Schwartz said.

"Right this minute!" said Skinner. Then he walked over to The Sevens and said that they were to leave. Immediately.

Even though we were coatless in the bitter cold, we dragged our heels getting down to the limo. We were looking over our shoulders at the red-brick house, the front porch illuminated by mobile spotlights.

In his brown flannel suit, striped cotton shirt, and silk tie, with the square cotton pocket handkerchief, Deem appeared there like someone yanked out of a PBS–TV play and pushed into the set of a cops-and-robbers sitcom. He had his hands up. He was smiling grimly.

"Is his daughter in there, too?" Schwartz asked me.

"No. But she's all right."

"What in the hell was going on, Fell? Did Dragon try to run off with her?"

Dr. Skinner said, "Get in back, boys! You'll have ample opportunity to discuss this on The Hill! Ready, Lieutenant?"

Hatch was looking over his shoulder too, in time to see Lowell Hunter follow Deem. All four of us were standing by the limo gawking.

Then Skinner said to the lieutenant, "I don't have a driver. You sit up front with me."

We got in, reluctantly.

Skinner leaned around to say, "I'm going to put up this window, but I advise you boys not to try collaborating on any story to shield Sevens! I've had my fill of Sevens skulduggery! . . . I'll put the heat on. Fell, you're shivering."

He didn't have to tell me that. My teeth were chattering.

The glass partition between the front and the back seats went up, and soon after we began gliding down Jericho, I felt the warm air.

Schwartz said. "Lauren and I couldn't figure out what happened to you. Kidder said you took off after the Deem girl like a bat out of hell."

"I did." I was beginning to feel all the fear I hadn't dared feel for my own poor ass. Fear, then the fatigue coming in with the relief that it was over.

"Skinner doesn't know it, but *I* called the police," Schwartz said. "I told them to call Deem. They said the phones were out here, that something was going on down here, but they didn't know what. And Saturday night—most of their cars are out looking for impaired drivers. . . . They said they were going to radio them over to Jericho, where you were, probably. . . . How did they know that, Fell?"

The yawn came moaning out of me. I couldn't help it. It was the delayed sound of panic or relief, all that was left from a frustrated scream, probably.

Schwartz gave me a look. "You're a cool one, Fell."

"Far from it."

Schwartz continued, "We figured you two Sevens could use some help maybe. We were warned not to go into the house, so I said we'd do a little street theater outside and see what happened."

"I was never so glad to see you all! Thanks, Lion!"

"How did Creery's stepbrother get in on the act, Fell? And where's Eddie Dragon?"

I held one hand up. "Later. Not right now."

Schwartz gave my leg a punch. "See? I told you Fate arranges exits and entrances. . . . But I have to admit I never really thought Dragon would pull something like this!"

Another punch, that time to my arm. "We came through for you, though, Fell!"

Whatever Schwartz imagined had been going on at the Deems', it had him bubbling over. "That Deem!" He laughed. "Did you see him come out? Nothing ruffles our boy, does it? He looked like he was coming out of church on a Sunday morning."

"Since when do you come out of church with your hands up?" I said.

"The police didn't mean for Deem to do it. And I think they got Hunter confused with Dragon. . . . But I never liked the looks of Lowell Hunter. Guys in their thirties with white hair make me nervous."

"How about guys seventeen with white hair?" I said. "I think mine's turning white after tonight."

"Not you, Fell. You're too nervy."

I put my head back against the leather seat and shut my eyes. I didn't want to think about Nina, but it was hard not to. Not to imagine her face when she found out about her dad. Not to wonder how she'd deal with that, and with the stunt Dragon had played on her: making her think her dreams had come true, he was whisking her away with him . . . and she'd worn that white dress, the kind a bride would choose.

Schwartz was humming a familiar tune.

What was it . . . Something about your voice calling . . . something right on the tip of my tongue.

Then he was whistling it softly.

Heavenly shades of night are falling—
it's Twilight Time,
Out of the mist your voice is calling—
it's Twlight Time.

I opened my eyes and turned my head to see his face.

"Yes, Fell, that's for you," he said. "You owe Sevens a Twilight Truth."

"*I* do?"

"You do. Because you *are* nervy, Fell. . . . You never should have attended The Charles Dance as Damon Charles. That's disrespectful, Fell. We don't make fun of our founder!"

"You're not kidding, either," I said.

"I don't kid about Sevens," said The Lion.

He wasn't the only Sevens who felt that way. Until I went home for Easter vacation, that song was whistled at me through my door, on campus, in the dining room at The Tower—wherever I passed another Sevens.

By the time I got back from Brooklyn, no one was whistling anymore. Maybe because of what happened at the end of those nine days.

I spent them cooking for Mom and Jazzy, and walking around God's country. Down to the Brooklyn Bridge, and across to the Promenade with its great view of the New York skyline. Up to the Botanic Garden, where the Japanese cherry trees were in bloom, and over to the Brooklyn Museum.

In Carroll Gardens I dropped in to see my grandfather

in the nursing home and listen to him tell me again why he was named after Theodore Roosevelt.

One night I made a lot of telephone calls until I connected with Nina. She was staying with her aunt Peggy up in Hartford, Connecticut.

"I'm glad you called, Fell," she said. "I thought you'd be mad at me. He's called too, Eddie has. We're friends now. Just good friends."

We didn't talk about her father. She didn't seem to want to, and neither did I.

At the end of our conversation I said I hoped we'd be good friends too, and Nina said she'd like that.

"Am I a good friend?" Jazzy asked me after I'd hung up.

"Yes."

"Then do I get Mr. Mysterious if I'm a good friend?"

I sat her down and talked about gift giving with her for a while. "Sometimes the best gifts are ones you don't ask for," I told her.

"But I like to know what I'm getting, Johnny. I always know what I want."

"Don't you ever want something money can't buy?"

"Like what?"

"Well, what we were just talking about. Friends."

"Girlfriends or boyfriends?"

"You can't buy either kind. You can't buy a true friend."

"What's a true friend?"

How did I answer her? I don't remember. But whatever I said only reminded me of Dib. What had happened between us was all my fault. I'd left him out. I'd become too full of myself and Sevens. Dib had been right that morning he'd told me that *I* was the one impressed by the gold 7. Mom hardly ever wore it, even with the head charms hanging beside it.

Going back to The Hill on the train, I came upon the newspaper story about David Deem's death. Out on bail, he was found in his Lincoln shot seven times through the heart. Neighbors heard the gun go off at five in the afternoon. . . . At twilight, I thought.

> Police have not determined yet if the dead rat found between his teeth has some tie-in with underworld ritual. Purportedly he had no Mafia connections.
>
> Lowell Hunter, alleged to be kingpin behind the DOT operation, has been held without bail charged with the murder of his stepbrother, Cyril Creery.

The Hill was buzzing with rumors about the three murders, Deem's in particular, because of The Sevens Revenge.

Since everyone in Sevens House had been on Easter vacation, far from Cottersville, it was being whispered that an alumnus had caught up with David Deem.

But Schwartz insisted it was someone with connections to Hunter. Someone who wanted Deem silenced, and chose to make it look like The Revenge.

There were stern notices posted everywhere on bulletin boards, insisting that more than ever now, Gardner had to put the past behind it.

Gossip, innuendo, rehashing of our crises, can only do grave injury to the future of the school! Do not look back. Go forward.

That was my intention when I went down to the dorm late in the afternoon, after I'd unpacked.

Dib was coming out as I was heading up the walk.

"I want to talk, Dib."

"Not now, Fell. I'm going out to dinner."

I walked along with him, toward the familiar green Mustang parked at the curb.

"How come Little Jack's driving? I thought he was pulled over on a DWI?"

"You know, Fell, I'd worry more about your crowd than mine. You could end up with a big mouse in your mouth."

I let that go. "Let's get together tomorrow," I said.

"Maybe. If there's time."

Little Jack rolled down the window and gave me a salute. "Aye, aye, sir!" he said.

I walked up closer. "What's that supposed to mean?"

"Aren't you giving my boy some orders, Fell?"

Dib said, "He doesn't give me orders." He went around to get in the passenger seat.

"I thought he did," said Little Jack.

He smelled of beer or whiskey; maybe both.

"You're in great condition to drive," I said.

"Cork it, Fell!" Dib shouted at me.

"Dib, he's *drunk*!"

"Dib"—Little Jack made what I'd said into a high whine—"he's drunk!"

I should have gone around, opened the door, and yanked Dib out.

That was what I told myself as I stood there while Little Jack took off, waving at me. "Bye-bye, Felly!"

Dib was staring straight ahead.

I watched the car weave down the street toward the hill.

Little Jack Horner
Sat in a corner.

I couldn't remember the rest of the nursery rhyme that began humming in my head, not then and there. Just those two lines.

But later on it came back to me. All that long, sad spring it did.

Then, when summer came, I went looking for Little Jack.

Oh, yes. *He* was still around.